Down
at the
End
of the
River

Down
at the
End
of the
River

Stories by Angus Woodward

Donaldsonville, Louisiana

Published by Margaret Media, Inc.
Copyright © 2008 Angus Woodward

ISBN: 978-0-9616377-6-7

The stories in this collection are works of fiction. Names, characters, and incidents are the products of the author's imagination or are used fictitiously. Any resemblance to actual events or persons, living or dead, is entirely coincidental.

Printed in the USA
by Sheridan Books, Chelsea, Michigan

Library of Congress Control Number: 2008920899

Margaret Media, Inc.
618 Mississippi St.
Donaldsonville, LA 70346
(225) 473-9319
www.margaretmedia.com

for Jalan

Acknowledgments

I'm grateful to the Louisiana Division of the Arts for financial support and to my employer, Our Lady of the Lake College, for creating a supportive atmosphere that values creative output. Thanks to my classmates and teachers in the MFA program at LSU for giving me the critical perspective to create these stories. The editors of six journals generously made room for these stories in their publications: *Xavier Review* ("Down at the End of the River," as "Captivated"), *Dominion Review* ("The Story of Jane and George"), *Louisiana Literature* ("Qatar Is an Emirate"), *Habersham Review* ("The Ride"), *Talking River Review* ("Don't Put Me Down"), and *Pennsylvania English* ("Out There in TV Land"). I want to thank Mary Gehman of Margaret Media for envisioning this book. My deepest gratitude goes to Jalan, Geneva, and Nina for continual moral support.

Down at the End of the River: Stories

Table of Contents

Down at the End of the River

One day I guess I decided it was foolish for a man my age to keep pestering people and I just stopped what I had been doing for practically forty years or something, not that I ever counted that carefully. No more breaking, no more entering. I vowed to toss the Coke-machine keys in the river the next time I was down in the Quarter. I couldn't bring myself to give away all of the guns, but planned to call some of my old assistants and ask if they wanted some, saving out a shotgun, three revolvers, and my thirty-ought-six just for security and holidays.

So what do I do now? I wondered, and gave the old TV a try. Nothing but a bunch of yahoos beeping and tussling on all those newfangled talk shows. I cracked the blinds to get a look at what other people were doing. The street was quiet and shady like always, but instead of thinking it was the boringest place on earth, I saw how peaceful and homey it was. Why would I want to run off to Fat City strip joints or out to the truck-stop casinos when I could do what my neighbors did on evenings like this? None of them were doing it just then, but often with the men home from work for the evening and two hours of daylight to go, people would find excuses to get out into their little yards, maybe to poison some fire ants or prune their azaleas, of which mine were halfway covering the windows. Doo-dad would be out soon with his glass of whiskey or can of beer, just sitting on the front step calling out smart comments to those who walked by. Because he was old like me, everyone thought his remarks were cute, but I knew better.

Next thing I knew I was out on my little concrete front porch with the intention of poking around in the garage to find a shovel or some other excuse to be outside, but before I took two steps I caught sight of the Heberts' house across the street and it cast a spell on me. I got rooted to the spot, staring at the house and reminiscing about the phase of my life that had just ended, especially that glorious day when Hebert came over maybe four years ago, said he and the wife were taking the motor home out to Utah to see the grandkids, be gone three weeks, someone coming on Wednesdays and Sundays to water the plants, mail stopped, just wanted to tell me so I could keep an eye on the place. This was when I was new to the neighborhood, and all the guys my age thought I was like them, thought I liked golf and *Reader's Digest*, thought I had plaid pants in the closet and liked to tinker with lawn mowers.

So a few days after he leaves I walk up to Hebert's side door and jimmy it in nothing flat. I go in through the kitchen, pluck the Sedan deVille keys off the key rack, check the freezer for steaks but it's mostly Light'n'Hearty TV dinners. The living room is the stopper-- huge television, jazzy stereo system with all kinds of lights and buttons. "I'll be back for y'all," I tell the electronics, and bump right into the piano. Baby grand, shiny new. A grandfather clock stands in one corner, and I think of that antique shop down on Royal where they won't ask questions. In the dining room I consider the crystal, but decide that even with Romano to help me it would be too much trouble, too fragile. The bedrooms are in the back. One has a nice ceiling fan but not much else, but the master bedroom is another story. The gun is easy to find in the nightstand, and I pocket it right then and there. A mint condition .45 semiautomatic. Closet number one is disappointing, all pastel pants and comfortable shoes, but there's an old sable jacket in her closet and a couple of strands of gold. The gold I grab, but mostly I'm taking notes, figuring how much truck Romano and I will need when we come back next week and load up the TV, stereo, piano, clock, and jacket, which is what we do, only we wind up taking the crystal too and even rolling up the living room Persian. For the time being I make a few calculations, then head out for a two-day joyride in the Caddy before I bring it to a guy I know out near the airport. When Hebert comes back, he says Did you notice any suspicious characters hanging around or hear any weird noises? I tell him, without lying, that I didn't.

That was the last time I did a neighborhood job myself. I got a little smarter and sent Romano alone when the good folks next door, the Tates, took their vacation to Bermuda. Same with the Richards on the other side, who took a cruise to Mexico with their favorite daughter.

I was standing there on the porch wondering what kind of stuff old Hebert had in there now when a UPS truck passed, blocking my view of Hebert's house just long enough to break the spell, which had held me there for a good five minutes. I shook my head, reminding myself that those days were over, especially since Hebert had double-barrel deadbolts and an alarm system put in as soon as he came back from Utah and saw that he had been cleaned out. I trudged back to the garage, where I found some rusty old pruning things on the floor, then went to chopping away at those big azaleas in front of my house, soon finding it made me sweaty and hardly changed the way the yard looked, except that now I had bunches of leaves and twigs strewn all over the grass. I glanced over Doo-dad's way and there he was, sitting out on his steps with his elbows on his knees, whiskey glass clutched in two hands. Dr. Doofus, his across-the-street neighbor, stood on the front walk with his whiskey glass, laughing about something Doo-dad had said. The sun was getting low and maybe being thirsty had something to do with it, but you would not believe the way those glasses were glinting at me. They were four doors down, but I could tell that Doo-dad had cracked the ice with a spoon so that there were chunks and slivers and the golden whiskey nestled down in it, with the sun shooting through as they shook their glasses the way people do, and I could hear that tinkling sound, too. Doo-dad and I went way back, what with him starting at NOPD about the time I commenced all of my carrying on, though I had only taken to calling him Doo-dad when he retired and started wearing deck shoes and dentures. I figured I might as well tell him I had just retired myself, and maybe I'd get a glass of whiskey as congratulations.

"Here comes Mush-mouth," Doo-dad told Dr. Doofus as I lumbered down the sidewalk, and by the glint in his smartass eyes I could tell he knew I had heard him.

I stopped in front of them. They looked at me, then at each other, making no move to say hello. "I decided to retire today," I told Doo-dad.

He snorted.

"What line of work you in, buddy?" Dr. Doofus asked. Most everybody on the street figured I had robbed my neighbors, thanks mainly to Doo-dad, who had pointed out the circumstantial evidence. Dr. Doofus was like the others, too chickenshit to act as if he knew what kind of a guy I was.

"Merchandising," Doo-dad said. "You move a lot of merchandise, don't you?"

"I'm an entrepreneur," I said. "But I just retired. Today."

Doo-dad snorted again. "It'll be a short retirement," he laughed. "You'll be moving more of that merchandise of yours by the weekend."

"What type of whiskey is that?" I asked hopefully.

"Not the type I give to little girls. How about a Piña Colada?"

"Ah, stuff your whiskey," I told Doo-dad and gave Dr.

Doofus a glare that killed his smirk. On the way back to my house I heard them laughing and wanted to come right back with a nine-millimeter in each hand. I had never used my guns to commit a crime, though, and wasn't about to start. My specialty was always sneaking in and sneaking out, with a little Coke-machine empty-ing and auto theft on the side. Guns made me feel safe, and every now and then you've got to show one to somebody to make him go away. Instead of heading in for the guns, I dug up a rake in the back of the garage and worked on getting the azalea trimmings shoved up under the bushes. I'd show them how straight I could go.

There was a serious party going on at Romano's apart-ment when I called him the following afternoon. Bunch of prim-itive music thumping in the background, and some chick who kept shrieking, "Ooh, that's wicked, Donny!"

"Mr. Randy, you got to come over!" Romano yelled, once he finally figured out who he was talking to.

"I got some guns you might want," I told him. "Come get them when you can, you hear?"

"Guns? Sure!" Romano whooped, then I heard a clatter like he'd dropped the receiver. The music got louder, and no mat-ter how I shouted no one came back to the phone. Finally I just listened to forty people hooting and hollering and crunching on potato chips, saying "Try some of this," and "Want to go upstairs for a minute?"

I boxed up the guns for Romano and set them by the door, thought about getting a gun cabinet for the ones I'd saved out for self-defense and New Year's Eve. I felt better knowing those weapons would be out of the house soon, because they had like a voodoo influence-- with them around I couldn't help think-ing like the criminal I had been for forty-some-odd years. For ex-ample, I knew it was the perfect time of day to hit the vending machines I had keys to, and it was hard not to want to cruise on down to the Quarter and gather a few of those nice hefty sacks of change. Doo-dad's sour face came to mind, and I grabbed the keys up out of the kitchen drawer with a different plan. I would go to the Quarter, but only to park, and I would walk over to the levee and let the river take those keys.

I fired up the Caprice and without thinking took my usual detour through the neighborhood, always a good way to see who was in and who was out, who had a furniture store truck pulled up in their driveway, who had left the trunk open while they ran in to get the phone. I had picked up a good many sacks of groceries that way. I won't take this detour anymore, I thought, taking that detour one last time.

There was this pair of lady gym teachers that lived right behind Doo-dad, and my eye had always been drawn by the one little window in the front of the house, shaped like a stop sign or something, and the way it was covered by a curtain made me curious, made me want to know what was inside the house where the two lady gym teachers lived. I let the car slow down and drift to the curb without thinking, and I sat there staring at that curtain, which was made of some of that real thin material, the kind you can almost see through, wrinkled on purpose into a kind of design. The window was like an eye, a magician's eye, and I stared at it, getting hypnotized and everything, imagining the picture on the wall across from the window, a painting of a naked lady getting out of a bathtub, or maybe some Egyptian thing. Not that I was ever interested in paintings. But below the painting I could imagine a piece of furniture, a hutch or maybe a sideboard, with drawers and a top and a cabinet part at the bottom. If I was to open the drawer on the left, there'd be a whole row of silver forks and knives stacked up nicely in soft velvety little compartments, and taking a spoon from the spoon slot, I turn it over and it says "Sterling." My jacket has plenty of big pockets, and I weigh them down with this delicious metal. Look, though-- where's that door lead to? In the bedroom I notice there's just one bed, a big one, but it's not my business what people do behind their closed doors, and lady gym teachers aren't known for wearing much in the way of earrings and necklaces, but they do have grandmothers, and that little mini chest on the dresser is where they keep their grandmothers' heirloom jewelry. It's a big little jewelry chest, with seven or eight drawers. I start at the top, and would you look at the bracelets? Diamond tennis bracelets for starters, and some chunky gold things. Now this second drawer is where they keep the earrings, and these here might be diamond, might not, no time to check and plenty of room in the pockets. Regular rings are just falling out of the next drawer, some nice gold bands and ones with stones, possible emeralds, a definite diamond or two. Into the pocket they go, and I'm getting that nice loaded-down feeling, the goods pulling at my jacket so I feel it in my shoulders.

As long as I'm in the bedroom I open the closet, and there are the videos, just like I figured. As far as I can tell they're all lesbo tapes, judging by the titles, but guys go in for that kind of thing too, and I think I might be able to unload a few somewhere. No one would believe the whips and chains and even weirder stuff in that closet, either, which I try not to touch. Just as I'm starting to push the closet doors closed, I see a lockbox on the floor, shoved up behind their running shoes. I pull the lockbox forward, and it makes a nice heavy scraping sound. One good shot with this weird billy-club thing hanging in the closet between the whips and the chains, and that lock's a goner. Why, the box itself might be worth something. If it turns out to be full of birth certificates and cucumber seeds I'll just dump it out and take it with me. But it's not full of paper and seeds. Well, it is full of paper-- green paper, though. Green and black. Who knows where lady gym teachers get cash like that, but what does it matter? It's cash-- fives, tens, and twenties in easy-to-pocket little bundles.

Maybe the government gives a special subsidy to freaks and perverts, which wouldn't surprise me these days. There's nothing sweeter than slipping an inch of twenties into the inside pocket of your very own jacket. It's a natural motion, to me. I don't even have to look. I just lift the lapel and slide the money right into the pocket.

The whole story just played through my head like a movie, but then I heard a car coming, and it broke the spell. My eye left the stop-sign shaped window and went right to my rearview. Here came one of the lady gym teachers in her Japanese Corvette, turning at the end of the street, and she rushed at my Caprice then slowed way down, and instead of pulling into her driveway she swerved past me and I got a look at her as she glanced over her shoulder with a mean look on her face. She just about tore up the road getting out of there, and turned the corner on two wheels, practically. I just knew she was going over to Doo-dad's house. I figured I'd tell anyone who asked that I had been doing a crossword puzzle, not even thinking about the lady gym teachers' house, and it's a free country and that's why the pilgrims came over here, or I'll just ask them, Is there a law against parking out in front of a lady gym teacher's house? Is there even a law against thinking about robbing someone, having a little daydream, or is this Russia or something?

It was evening time when I got back from the river, where I had thrown my Coke-machine keys as far as I could off the top of the levee. They landed in the busted up concrete and trash down next to the river, which must have been further away than it looked. I came straight home, and before I could get from the curb to the front door, Doo-dad came charging down the sidewalk toward me. "She told me what you were doing!" he yelled.

"I wasn't doing anything," I groaned.

He came up close, close enough that I worried he might

take a swing at me. "You've terrorized this neighborhood long enough," he said quietly, sticking out his soft old chin. "But I'm not the only one who's got one of these." He pulled his hand from his pocket and waved something in my face, too close for me to make out what it was. Not until he slipped it back into his pocket did I see the bullets snug in their places and realize he'd brandished the clip from his pistol.

"Get off my property." I turned my back on him and marched right into the house, letting the door slam behind me. I stared at the old brass umbrella stand for a moment, wanting to tell Doo-dad that I was like him now, that soon I would start edging the lawn regularly and hosing down the driveway every evening, that he didn't need to be so ready to attack all the time. Not that his house was not worth breaking into-- I had seen all the power tools he had wedged into his garage, had seen him and his wife Beverly come back from estate sales with boxes full of treasure.

I never would have figured that Doo-dad would turn into a leaf-raking, estate-sale-going, pink-shirt-wearing old man. Back in the day, I knew him as Officer Saucier, and he was known for being enthusiastic with the billy club when he came across a dice game or a shoving match between two drunks. He collared me plenty of times, though I normally had a big enough tip on someone else that he let me go after a night or two. After what I saw at dawn one day outside the station, he started to look the other way no matter what I did.

I was up early knocking off parking meters. It had rained the night before, and steam was rising off the street already, what with the July heat being so fierce. Here came Officer Saucier around the corner. I had a bag of change tied to my belt and a meter hanging open in front of me, but I just leaned on the wall and raised my cigarette to my lips. I knew how to look as if I had nothing to do with what was going on. Lucky for me, a car came roaring up to Officer Saucier, and Beverly jumped out. I watched them talking for a few moments; then Beverly's voice swooped up loud enough for me to hear: "But she needs me to go out there, Vaughn. Something's wrong with the baby, and she don't have no one else." Then he said something, shaking his head, and she jumped in with, "I don't care what you say--" He cut her off by raising his fist. Just raising it and holding it above his shoulder. Her arms jerked up in front of her face, and she sort of quivered there, waiting. He pointed at the car and she scrambled in, then slid over for him to drive. As he settled in behind the wheel, Saucier spotted me, froze. Beverly was crying. I flicked the cigarette, pushed off from the wall, and scooped the change out of the open meter into my bag. Saucier looked at me hard as he drove past, but I looked back just as hard and kept on scooping.

Romano came at a bad time, right after I put on my pajamas. I opened the door, and there he stood in a cloud of moths and June bugs, hair all frizzy and wild. "Mr. Randy!" he hooted. "I come to see you!"

"All right," I sighed, pulling him through the door before he woke up the neighbors. "Come on."

"Nice pajamas, Mr. Randy!" he laughed, then switched to that polite-boy-next-door attitude I've seen him use. "Nice house, too, Mr. Randy. I really like it." He nodded seriously at the old curtains, the screwed-up couch. "And hey, I forgot what a tasty neighborhood you had around here, Mr. Randy."

"Here are your guns." I shoved at the box with my foot.

"Ooh, all right. Yeah." He squatted down and started to paw through the miscellaneous collection of old revolvers, semi-automatics-- a few .32's, a bunch of .38's, a good many .45's and the two nine-millimeters. "Hey, mind if I just sell some of these?"

"Sell them, use them, whatever," I said. "Just don't say who gave them to you."

He stood up with his arms wrapped around the box, grinning happily. "Oh, right, no way."

"Okay. So good night."

"Good night. Thanks again." He didn't move.

"Let me get the door for you," I hinted.

"Hey, Mr. Randy, " Romano said, "I got an idea for a job. You want to do a job with me?"

"I don't do jobs anymore, Romano."

"Oh, right. Giving your guns away. Okay, I'll see you around, Mr. Randy."

I wasn't exactly awake, but I wasn't exactly dreaming, either. It started with me thinking about the way the knob on my front door hung sort of loose and I never used the deadbolt, and on the side door it would be easy to break the glass and reach in to unlock it. I should have left the porch light on. Who the hell would notice a man sneaking up onto my porch, especially with the azaleas too high? And if they did notice, they'd probably figure it served me right and not do a thing to stop it. I could just see the way he would push the door open slowly, barely enough to slip in. Then he's in the kitchen, looks at the dead houseplant in the window and the exploded remains of the hot dog I tried to microwave in a coffee mug, frowns at the piled up trash can in the corner. He moves carefully in the faint light from the street, barely lifting his feet, puts a hand on the doorframe and peers around into the living room. Tin foil on the TV antenna, sagging couch, too many old newspapers stacked under the coffee table. He thinks of digging under the sofa cushions, then hears me creaking the bed and snorting in my sleep. Eases the clip out of his pocket and clicks it into his .38. By this time I'm deep in a dream about golden locomotives and doughnut hills, so there's no chance I'll hear. Here he comes now, wincing when the hall floor squeaks as he tiptoes across to the door of my bedroom, wide open as always. He mouths the word "damn" at having to pick his way through the clothes and magazines on the floor. I can just picture the smug look he gets when he sees me lying there asleep with my mouth hanging open. He always was a conceited bastard. Maybe I would wake up as he stood over me, have a chance to say, "Saucier, you're taking it too far this time," but then it would be lights out. Blam.

Snap out of it, I told myself. I finally fell asleep, but instead of trains and doughnuts, I dreamed about being awake the next day, doing what I had to do to set things straight with Doo-dad. It was one of those nights where you think that you are doing whatever it is you're going to do the next day, and then you dream that you wake up and say, "That's funny, I just dreamed about the thing that I am about to do," and then you dream again that you are doing it, but now you are even more convinced that you are actually doing it. If you manage to start dreaming about robbing a bank and having a beautiful relationship with the lovely young teller or something, eventually your dream self remembers that you are supposed to be doing this other thing, and you dream of driving across town through crazy traffic in a big rush to do the other thing, which in my case was marching right down to Doo-dad's house at first light to say, "Listen, damn it, I just gave away all my guns and Coke-machine keys and I am not a criminal anymore, so stop acting like you never did anything bad in your life and give me a chance, or do you want to have it out right here, man to man?"

I had rolled in from the truck stops and strip joints at dawn enough times to know that Doo-dad would be outside at first light, either waiting for his little terrier to poop in the grass or sweeping up any little leaf or stick that had fallen onto his driveway or sidewalk during the night. Of course, it being Saturday, there was the chance that he and Bev would have their eye on some juicy estate sale, in which case they might already be gone, off across town somewhere lined up outside someone's door, jockeying for position with the other estate-sale freaks. How would they feel if they came home and found half their dishes smashed and all that silver and gold they've been hoarding long gone, with me halfway to Cuba? I don't do that anymore, I thought, but also thought if the jackpot of a lifetime presented itself I might have to grab it.

A gang of noisy sparrows scrambled from one crape myrtle to the next as I walked, but otherwise nothing moved out on the street at six o'clock that morning. No sign of Doo-dad on the sidewalk, and I got all set to take a seat on his front steps until he came out, only I noticed the door stood a half-foot open. I sat down anyway, figuring he might have run in for the broom or some sort of special dog shovel, but my heiney had hardly touched the concrete when I heard a voice coming from inside, and the skin on the back of my neck crawled because the voice wasn't Doo-dad's or Bev's.

You would not believe the amount of stuff they had packed into that house. Right inside the door they had a skinny table, and it was covered with little china people and animals surrounding an ancient metal lamp. My fingers wiggled as I passed, trying to tell me how easy it would be to pocket a peacock or a greyhound and suggesting that maybe I deserved a couple of free trinkets, given the situation, but I just kept going. I glanced into the kitchen as I hurried past, saw shelves lining the walls, and fancy glasses and china plates with paintings on them covered those shelves. There was a big picture of a mountain over the couch in the living room, and it looked like you could hardly walk in there for all the furniture and fancy chairs and tables covered with decorations, but I decided to just keep heading toward that voice because now that I was closer I could hear not what it was saying but the angry, bossy sound of it. I moved as fast as I could without making noise, a quick tiptoe. You should have seen the dining room though, all shiny wood furniture and fancy dishes and wooden boxes that looked like they could have been full of silverware. Those boxes pulled like magnets drawing me into the room, and for a moment I stood frozen in place. "What about the attic?" the voice demanded, and I broke away from the dining room.

I sidled up to the half-open bedroom door and peeked in. Doo-dad and Bev knelt on the floor next to their bed, still in their pajamas. Bev was crying all bent over, but Doo-dad was straight as a tree, looking right up at Romano. "I bet you got a safe in here somewhere, too," Romano was saying, waving one of my nine-millimeters all over the room. Like I said before, I never used a gun to steal anything, but even I knew better than to look all around while you've got a gun on somebody, especially when that somebody is Doo-dad and he's about two feet from his night-stand drawer.

"Get out," I yelled, barging in, and Romano whirled, putting both hands on the gun and pointing it right at me. Doo-dad eased his hands around in front of himself.

"Stop moving," Romano shouted, putting the gun on Doo-dad again.

"Get the hell out!" I bellowed, and Romano gave me this wide-eyed, tilted-head look.

"But Mister--"

I waved my arm at him. "Go on, now!"

He finally took my advice, only because he didn't know what else to do. He walked out of the bedroom all cocky, stuffing the nine-millimeter into his waistband. Doo-dad eased the drawer open as quick as could be and pulled out his .38. "He's got a gun!" I called.

"I noticed that," Doo-dad growled, and jumped out into the hall, firing twice, but Romano was already running. All Doo-dad did was shoot two slugs into his own front door. He ran out into the street pretty quick, then came hobbling back in like an old man, which is what he is. I went to have a seat in the dining room to give Bev a chance to pull herself together, only they had so much stuff packed in there I couldn't pull out a chair. Bev came out with a housecoat clutched around her and a Kleenex in each hand. "Come on," she said, and I followed her to the kitchen. Doo-dad joined us while she was gathering coffee mugs and fiddling with the coffeemaker. He set the gun on the table and sat down, shaking his head.

"I'd better go," I said.

"No, wait." Doo-dad stood up and opened the cabinet over the sink, taking out two fancy cut-glass tumblers. "I usually don't start until at least noon," he said. I watched him put ice between two dish cloths and bang at it with an old hammer. The whiskey came out of a glass-fronted cabinet in the dining room. He brought mine to me and sat down on the other side of the kitchen table. Bev leaned on the counter near her machine, waiting as it coughed and burbled.

"How does it feel to be one of the good guys?" Doo-dad asked, giving me a look.

I held my glass up in front of the window so a slice of early-morning sun shone through it and said, "I'd sure like to know."

The Ride

Air Conditioning

Outside, summer was in full effect, the humid air absorbing sunlight, cloaking everyone in syrupy heat. His exposure to summer was always brief—in his driveway every morning and evening, short jaunts across the deck of the parking garage at work. He'd never really believed that breathing processed air was harmful or that sudden changes in temperature surprised the heart. It was more that he'd been seeing the city through glass—in his car as he drove to work, or from his office window three stories up. He felt too removed, isolated, privileged. I wasn't always like this, he thought, remembering the year he'd lived in an uptown apartment cooled only by ceiling fans. He'd walked everywhere. Now the only strangers he ever encountered were separated from him by windows. So it was not quite on impulse that he parked his car near the old apartment on his way to work and stepped out into the tropical morning to stand at a streetcar stop.

Boarding

An elderly couple in brand new white shorts stood close together conferring over a map of the city. He listened as they wondered what would be worth seeing. The next time he glanced up the street to look for the car he found a young woman standing near him. She was wearing a nurse's uniform and had appeared noiselessly. He smiled and wished her good morning. She smiled meekly. It made him feel better—when was the last time he'd spoken to someone like that? And he felt even better when he waved her and the white couple ahead of him as the car rumbled up, door opening and step folding down. "Move aside," the driver told him sullenly when he had to fish around for the right change after cheerfully asking how much it was these days. That was a minor setback, but he kept his chin up as three kids in private-school clothes crowded past him, slamming exact change into the coin slot.

Central Business District

His building was less than ten years old. It was tall, polished. From his window he had a glimpse of the river and a good view down the long straight street. Sometimes he sat thinking, watching the busy traffic, hustling pedestrians, loitering transients. From that height the city seemed frantic and useless. Sometimes he and his colleagues walked a block or two to an oyster house or deli, but the restaurant on the first floor was easier and just as good.

Distraction

It was fascinating to share space with so many strangers of so many different stations, to be breathing the same moist air, to listen to their talk. He'd forgotten how diverse this city was. He found himself staring. There were extremes of every kind—the oldest, the fattest, the darkest, the prettiest, the poorest. He watched them get on and off, tried to guess where they would sit.

Executives

He supposed he looked intimidating—to the black nurse at the car stop, for example. He'd forgotten that he wore a uniform of sorts, and that it colored others' perception of him. Standing there in a tie and a dark suit, his hair moussed perfectly, the big fine briefcase. Just about everyone he saw during the day wore the same uniform and he thought nothing of it, but these nurses, students, laborers weren't used to it. Some of them probably hated him.

Flow

The streetcar was like a vessel into which water seeped and from which it leaked. There was a gradual change in the composition of the crowd as riders got off and others boarded. The diversity of earlier was diluted as they traveled further into the city. The crowd became younger and darker. Soon the old tourists were the only other whites on the car. He wondered why and it bothered him not to understand.

Greeting

A whole crowd of young men grew in the section ahead. They boarded one or two at a time but seemed to recognize one another immediately. He watched how they clasped hands and slapped at each other in a complex ritual. It happened too fast for him to pick out its separate elements, a dance. He wanted to learn it.

Harold

Most of them wore black hats with silver X's embroidered on the front. He thought maybe that identified them as members of the same gang. No wonder they were so instantly familiar with each other. One of the first ones to step aboard wore a dark blue work shirt with his name stitched over the pocket. He didn't look anything like a Harold, at least not like any of the Harolds he'd ever seen. He'd roomed with a Harold one year at college, and he was more what you'd expect— brainy, thick glasses, walking with a gawky sort of brawn. This Harold looked tough, like all the members of his gang. He kept his eyes half lidded and if he laughed he laughed coldly. He'd walked to his seat carelessly and slowly.

Watching, he sensed that the others greeted Harold a little nervously, deferred to him, laughed hardest when he was amused.

Isolation

The old tourists stepped off uncertainly at Lee Circle just as the driver was about to start again. They stood on the sidewalk, one peering up at the statue, the other fighting the unfolded map. The car was suddenly less crowded than it had been a few blocks ago, and now he was the only white. Why? There were whites driving alongside, whites on the sidewalk. The gang seemed to get louder and more boisterous, arguing hilariously about some game. All other riders were alone, squeezed up against the windows. His seat faced inboard and he couldn't help watching and listening. It seemed like maybe Harold caught him staring and muttered something unheard which made the rest roar. Some of them glanced at him as they laughed. He felt insulted and petrified.

Jaywalker

His stop was near the end of the line but it wasn't the end of the line, so he was a little alarmed when five or six of the young men stepped off behind him. Harold was one of them. The others seemed to hover around Harold, not starting after him until he'd made his move. This was the worst idea, he thought, hurrying around in front of the streetcar, trotting to cross as the Nissan coming at him blew its horn. He strode along in near panic, wondering how he'd stand the ride back to his car at the end of the day. Maybe he'd take a cab. As he pushed through the heavy glass doors of his building at last, relief and cold air hit him full force.

Knees

It was strange how fear seemed to reside in his legs. He'd kept his briefcase on his lap on the streetcar, and thinking back he realized he'd pushed it further out as the ride progressed. He hadn't hugged its solidity to him as you'd expect, but instead felt safer with his joints protected. Standing, he'd felt weak there, and his rush to the building hadn't been easy. In the lobby, the elevator, the halls, his legs strengthened and thickened, becoming more wooden.

Link

Moving through the office, wishing his underlings a good morning, squeezing the elbows of colleagues as he passed, nodding importantly, he felt good about his job, his position, just knowing all these people and being part of a community or at least a team. He felt at home. It had nothing to do with color, he decided. It had more to do with a simple human need to be among familiar faces and voices. It was almost physiological, maybe. Among any strangers your pulse quickens, temperature rises, muscles contract. Instinct gets you ready. But here with people he knew, he could be himself.

Meeting

Normally it would have been a bother, a disruption of his day, something that could possibly delay lunch. But today he was happy to remember that there would be a late morning meeting of some of his colleagues with four vice presidents from the Houston office. Not that he wanted to forget his voyage through the city exactly, but it would refresh his sense of place and belonging. And really the meeting could be enjoyable if everyone was in the right mood. Perhaps if he surrounded himself with comrades for long enough he'd be strengthened for the trip back to his car, steeled to face it.

Nobody

How many times recently had he been where not one person knew his name?

Organic

He got the feeling the meeting would be a good one, loose and jocular, by the way it began. At five till, he wandered over to the hall outside the conference rooms and found three of his colleagues joking by the door. He caught on to what they were saying as he walked up and slipped in a smart comment, producing a round of laughter. Others joined them and they waited past the hour, unconcerned. When the vice presidents showed up they gradually seeped into the conference room and began arranging themselves in no particular order around the table. No one got sour when they realized the room was too small and they'd have to go next door. They laughed, got up, kept talking, took their time.

Phalanx

Later he thought about how sudden and organized they must have seemed as they entered the larger conference room. In the hall someone mentioned lunch and a sense of purpose overtook them. He and another sprang forward to open the double doors for their visitors, who strode in first, followed closely by a double line of the others, all of them marching quickly around the table to their seats, startling a member of the maintenance crew who was at the window with a spray bottle, a squeegee and a cloth.

Quicken

No one paid much attention as the man fumbled with his supplies, ducking his head, glancing cautiously at them as he bent to retrieve the bottle he'd dropped. He tried to slip out completely unnoticed, but the room was narrow and suddenly crowded, all the chairs pulled out, and he had to stand obtrusively, waiting for everyone to sit down and pull up to the table.

Recognition

At first he only saw what the others saw: a stranger standing in their way, practically an extraterrestrial—his world was so alien, his clothes, language. But then he saw the blue work shirt and tried to place it, only wondering for a moment before his eyes fell on the name over the pocket. This was a different Harold, wasn't it? Not the insolent gangster. No hat, but it was him—same eyes, same cafe au lait complexion. He wanted to speak, to say something reassuring, but before he could one of the VPs glanced up and addressed Harold's sleeve, asking him to fill the water pitcher. Harold hooked the pitcher with one finger and squeezed his way out. His walk and posture were different, probably because of the way his knees had gone to water.

Suspension

The meeting began and progressed quickly while he sat studying his hand. Any moment and the door would open, Harold would re-enter. And how could he show him? He'd rise from his seat and take the pitcher from him, share the task. Or maybe a deeply felt thanks and a look in the eye would do it. His ear was tuned to the sound of the latch releasing and he didn't hear the voices around him, though he turned this way and that attentively, trying to appear to participate. He heard the vinyl seats shift, a pen drumming, papers lifted, briefcases snapped open.

Time

He kept listening. The meeting inched forward and no one came to the door. He started to descend into it, noticing the tumblers on the tray at one end of the table and the blank spot for the pitcher. Soon one of their visitors would wonder aloud what was taking so long and his colleagues would dutifully swear and belittle Harold. The second half of the meeting was endless and without meaning. He studied faces and imagined ways to excuse himself and go after Harold.

Unrehearsed

Despite the informal jokey air there was protocol to follow, almost a script for these meetings, even for the way they'd stood in the hall and the way they came out slowly, talking in small bunches. He was able to seem involved by sticking close, nodding thoughtfully. But when he saw a blue shirt and black hair down the hall he broke away without apologizing and strode toward the man. Hey, he said, tapping his arm. It was someone else, a much older guy who said, What you need? He couldn't think of a word to say.

Vanishing

He declined to join the visitors and his colleagues for lunch. Instead he retreated to his office and sent down for a sandwich. He tried to contemplate everything that had happened. It was strange—could he be getting sick and feverish? The entire world seemed to be based on a new premise, one he couldn't yet fathom. He wandered out to the coffeemaker and halfway there told himself to snap out of it before he got some kind of reputation. He did snap out of it an hour later, when a company rumor came true and one of his colleagues was fired. There was a lot of huddling, terse phone calls to make, schedules to reshuffle. He felt his strength coming back as he hustled to respond to the crisis and clarify his allegiances.

Waiting

Out of habit he stepped off the elevator at P3 and had taken four steps across the concrete when he remembered the events of the morning, distant now. He swore, laughed, and punched the elevator button. On the way down he resolved to use the streetcar at least once a week, thinking it might make things better in some small way. At the car stop he stood in front of a mother and her three children, tapping his fingers along the side of his briefcase. He shifted from one foot to the other, took a few steps this way then that, tried to find a spot on the concrete where he felt at ease. He'd only been there for maybe forty-five seconds before a green and yellow cab slowed at the curb, scanning. It was much easier to just raise his hand and trot after the taxi.

X

Where did those hats come from? he wondered. Come to think of it, he'd seen some on television. Were these gangs nationwide now? How could he have missed such a critical development?

Yack Yack Yack

You live uptown? the driver asked when he told him the intersection near where he'd parked. Before he could answer, the cabby began a stream of opinion about the area—Nice houses along St. Charles. You ever go to that one restaurant? Lot of college kids. More crime than there used to be. Blacks moved in and ruined it. Those coffee places went over big, didn't they? He wanted to break in, disagree, or at least silence the man. He knew he had to. He didn't.

Zero

It was wonderful to finally get into his car and take the controls. He felt like he'd been dragged around all day, a puppet on strings, tossed this way and that by strange events and feelings. He drove fast and arrived two minutes earlier than usual. His wife was out watching their son ride his trike on the driveway. The sight made him delirious. At dinner she sat smiling at him, helping their son eat without having to watch what she was doing. He told her about the rumor coming true. That was all he said about his day, because really nothing else had happened.

A Proclaimer in Creeperdom

Gary first met Liz in a hospital waiting room. Four minutes into their first conversation, he wished they were murmuring to one another in an obscure corner of the city's most iconoclastic coffee house over cups of Harsh Incan Brew or reclining on a grassy levee near Lake Pontchartrain spitting quiet words up into the sky. Instead he sat next to her on a vinyl chair that had been occupied by countless hemophiliacs and flu sufferers, studying her homely appearance under unkind fluorescent light. She was homely in the old-fashioned sense, lovely and reminding him of home, making him think he had been playing the part of CBD power-luncher for too long and needed to get back up to Lexington Parish where there were plenty of pure women like her.

He had interrupted her perusal of a tattered *Reader's Digest* by sitting down abruptly and asking, "Are you a Proclaimer?" Her angular smile had not electrified him half as much as the warm, familiar music of her voice as she confessed that she did not know what a Proclaimer was. "But you are from Lexington Parish, aren't you?" he asked.

Short nod. "Near Gardenia." He studied her further as she offered a careful pinpointing of her parents' home on Highway 334 just past the second bridge, not far from the old Hungarian cemetery. She was lovely in her modest knee-length dress, with no makeup and her straight honey hair tucked up in a bun.

Gary understood how tired he was of the city women with their rigid hair and lipstuck mouths. Liz's simple, chaste appearance reminded him of the women he had known in church as a young Proclaimer.

"I'm from Waltzer, myself," he offered, and set out to explain his first question. "But Proclaimers are-- I guess the official name was the Third Church of Christ, but most people called us the Proclaimers."

She seemed to shudder slightly at the name of his church, but she remained polite. "Why Proclaimers?"

"They believed that they could only truly live in Christ's spirit if they proclaimed his name each day, saying 'Jeeezzzusss' over and over again. There's a verse in maybe, um, First Thessalonians that they really zeroed in on." Again he noticed her squirming subtly.

"But it isn't done anymore?"

"Oh, it is. I just don't belong to the church anymore."

Liz drew back a little. "Do you go to church at all?"

If only they had been sharing the front seat of a small car zipping along River Road or strolling hand in hand along a carnival midway. But all they had was vinyl, fluorescence, and an audience of bored senior citizens feigning interest in *Better Homes and Gardens*. Given a more suitable ambiance, he would have told her what had happened at an interstate rest stop near Shreveport when he was nineteen. If there had been time and leisure, he may have been able to evoke the odor of diesel, the harsh sunlight, the stooped form of Minister Hayes, and the startling sight of a monstrous lavender bus pulling up alongside the church van at the rest stop. Minister Hayes had shaded his eyes, leaning back to read the giant airbrushed words along the fuselage of the motor coach: The Fifth Dimension. Ain't they some famous singin' group? he asked Gary. The bus popped open with a hiss, and five elaborately dressed gold-decorated celebrities sauntered forth. As the group headed toward the little restroom building, Minister Hayes pulled Gary close, whispering that here was a chance to spread the gospel word of Jeeezzzusss to those who could make quite a difference in the world. Gary politely protested that they were probably in a hurry; Minister Hayes assured him that it would not hurt to talk to them for a few minutes. Go on, he urged, as the quintet came back toward them. Gary's voice never seemed weaker or sillier than when he placed himself in their path and said, "Excuse me, do y'all believe in proclaiming the name of Our Savior?" To his surprise, they were curious and friendly. He explained that it was important to achieve maximum volume and depth, and to refrain from hurrying. "Real loud, low, and slow," he advised. They nodded, smiling, and Gary asked them to proclaim His name with him then. "Jeeezzzusss," he intoned, and a couple of them came in on the last syllable. "Come on, now. Loud, low, and slow," he repeated. "Jeeezzzusss," they all groaned. "That's good," Gary said, startled. "Again . . . Jeeezzzusss." All of them had clear, strong voices, and with the bald one's solid bass the results were astounding. "One more time," Gary murmured, and they breathed deeply. "Jeeezzzusss." They stopped, looked at each other. Two or three Dimensions shook their heads in amazement. "All right, man," one said, and they stepped toward their bus. Minister Hayes popped out of the van, spewing leaflets and talking a mile a minute about the church and its exact address and willingness to accept donations of any size. Suddenly the Fifth Dimension was in a rush, turning their backs on Minister Hayes to board the bus. Gary was never more embarrassed to be a Proclaimer, and it didn't help that Minister Hayes crowed about Gary's proclaiming with the Fifth Dimension all the way home and all the way through the week, even finding occasion to work it in to his next sermon. In the right circumstances, Gary might have been able to tell Liz how it all felt, and she might have seen why he had drifted away from the church during college. In a hospital waiting room, all he could tell her was, "Well, I haven't found the right church yet," as if he had been looking. "Which church do you go to?" he asked, more to change the subject than to invite himself into her life.

"Well, most outsiders call us the Creepers," she admitted.

Gary shrugged. "Haven't heard of it."

She smiled. "Maybe you should come to our service one Sunday."

"Maybe you should have dinner with me sometime," Gary countered.

She narrowed her eyes, still smiling. "Maybe if you come to the service, I'll go to dinner with you."

He managed to give her his card before her formidable mother came charging into the waiting area. "Geologist II," Liz read, and laughed. Then her mother towered over them, severe in a much tighter bun and antique glasses of the most utilitarian sort. "Oh, this is, um, Gary," her daughter said, gesturing toward him.

"Gary Larpenter." He shook her mother's doughy hand.

"Liz and I have got to skedaddle," her mother informed him sternly, as if to crush any notions he might have of eventually deflowering or holding the hand of her daughter. "My cousin Midge had her gall bladder zapped with a laser today, and we've got to get up to the seventh floor to see her." As they skedaddled, Gary noted that Liz moved with the hesitant grace of an egret: long neck and legs, every step carefully considered.

On the phone, Gary found out that the service would be at ten, that there was a sign, too small to be seen from the road, and that she did not live with her mother as he had feared. In fact, she had left Lexington Parish too, though she had only gone two parishes away to work as an insurance underwriter in Ponchatoula. This gave him some hope that she was more than just a Creeper, that they could soon get past talking about churches. She might even remove the pins from her hair once he took her beyond her mother's sphere of influence.

He felt a little too slick in his chambray shirt and power tie among the men in their white short sleeves and clip-ons, the women in floral dresses that allowed only their faces, hands, and stocking-clad calves to show. Fortunately, Liz drove in behind her mother before he had to spend too much time mingling with the other Creepers out in front of the church, where they stood chatting before the service. Her mother went straight inside, pausing only to shake his hand, call him Jerry, and complain of the hot sun. He found himself face to face with Liz, whose hair was a little more tightly wound now, and whose dress was very modestly cut but a blazing shade of blue. "I'm here," he managed to say.

"I'm so glad you came!" she exclaimed, because Lexington Parish women must exclaim such phrases. "Does this mean you're taking me to dinner?" she asked quietly, leaning toward him conspiratorially.

Gary wanted to take her hand and skip across the church yard, but he managed to rein himself in a little. "Let's drive down to Manchac as soon as this is over."

She nodded, and they joined the flow of church members now moving toward the building. He followed her between rows of simple wooden pews to a seat near the front, just behind her mother. The chapel was bare, with dusty, unfinished plank floors and whitewashed walls. After a few minutes, an elderly man in a gray suit rose from the first pew and shuffled forward, then positioned himself behind a podium that looked like it had been cast off by the local high school. "Let us pray," he croaked, and Gary bent his head with the congregation.

"Dear Gosh," the old man began, and Gary's eyes popped open. Speech impediment? he wondered. "We ask your blessing upon this church and those gathered here today, and that you may keep us from harm, especially with a holiday weekend approaching and so many drunks upon the roads. Golly, we know that you sent your Son to this world to wash us clean of sin, and pray that we may follow his example and never stray from the path you have chosen for us. Amen."

"Amen," Liz murmured, lifting her chin and fixing the minister with a clear gaze. Gary studied her for a moment, puzzling over the contrast between her complex face, with its long nose, full lips, strong brow, and the plain blank wall beyond.

The old man raised a tattered Bible from the podium and opened it, letting the cover flap against the wood. "In the life of Gee Whiz, we see many examples of the kind of life we should lead to preserve our souls from being danged to the fires of Heck."

Gary surreptitiously eyed those around him. Liz and her mother were perfectly attentive and serious. A fourteenish boy two rows ahead studied the ceiling dreamily, but otherwise everyone Gary could see was paying attention.

"In Jiminy's life we have a perfect model of how to behave," the minister was saying. "Why, if we could all be as polite and righteous as Cripes, the Dickens would have a deuce of a time corrupting this world."

Gary's confusion passed as he realized that he was not mis-hearing the minister's words, and that the others heard them too. In the absence of confusion, he embarked upon a mighty struggle to keep from laughing. He couldn't help smiling, and hoped anyone who noticed would assume he merely felt the joy of Golly's presence. The pressure to stay silent gnawed away at him, though, and he had to open his mouth or risk annihilation. First he yawned, then coughed. The fourteenish boy looked back at him curiously. Gary tried not to listen to the sermon, attempting to conjure a little anxiety over the presentation he would be making at work on Wednesday. It was not enough to distract him from the minister's passionate words. "Geez Louise gave his life for you, for crying out loud!" he exclaimed, and gave the podium a surprisingly fierce pounding with his fist. "Gosh gave his only Son! All this goes into why we must devote our lives to Criminy. Three forty-two."

The congregants abruptly rose to their feet, some fumbling with thick hymnals, and Gary jumped up. Liz smiled and held her hymn book open between them. *Nearer, my Gosh, to Thee; nearer to Thee. Even though it be a cross that raiseth me, still all my song shall be nearer, my Gosh, to Thee; nearer, my Gosh, to Thee, nearer to Thee.*

Am I in church? Gary wondered, as the preacher resumed his sermon. The physical surroundings reminded him of Minister Hayes' church, although the Proclaimers had relied more heavily on fluorescent lighting due to a low ceiling and the scarcity of windows. It was true that often when he thought of some of the highlights of his time with the Proclaimers he began to blush, embarrassed for his earlier self, who had felt no embarrassment. But sometimes he missed being nine, twelve, fourteen, when sitting in a church full of people moaning "Jeeezzzusss" together had given him the spooky, secure feeling of his spirit floating toward the ceiling. At the same time, he had known that everyone else in the room felt the same way. "Nearer, My God, to Thee" had really meant something then. Here in Liz's church he felt a little further from heaven than he did out in the world, where Jesus' name was on bumper stickers, and God's creatures and pine trees and waterways shined so stunningly. He strained his eyes to look at Liz without turning his head more than a few millimeters. Was she embarrassed, the way he had been embarrassed in the ninth grade when Hal Samson had slept over on a Saturday night and come to church with him the next day? Liz had a serene, pleased look that worried him.

"All Hail the Power of Jeepers' Name" was the closing

hymn, and at its conclusion Gary hurried past Liz, who had stopped to chat with a very short elderly lady. Bursting through the door, he was embraced by the searing, damp air, the blazing sunlight, the lush symphony of summer bug songs. He felt calmer, able to walk more slowly toward his car, deciding along the way that he would not just leave without speaking to Liz, that in fact he would wait for her, take her out as promised.

Gary's lunch with Liz would have been a success if not for his tactile encounter with a seafood platter. The waitress headed toward their table, and they both looked hungrily at the huge round tray she carried, loaded with his seafood platter, her fried catfish special, their tartar and cocktail sauces, cole slaws, fries. "Here we go," the waitress called happily, beginning to lower the tray from her shoulder. Gary saw her hand slip from the edge of the tray, saw her panicked face, and managed to turn away slightly and duck his head. Liz squealed. Seafood and french fries and sauces rained down upon his head, neck, and back. Later it would not seem possible, but he identified every piece of food as it hit him, differentiating between the hard peck of fried oysters on his scalp, the prickly slap of a battered soft-shell crab across one shoulder, and the bounce of boiled shrimp down his spine. Cole slaw delivered the final blow, slopping onto his collar before tumbling slowly down the back of his shirt.

The waitress knelt beside him. "Oh my God, oh my God, oh my God," she cried, making feeble attempts to scrape some of the food from the floor up onto the tray.

"Jeeezzzusss!" Gary exclaimed, wincing, afraid to move. Remembering Liz, he thought, "Here's where I look up and find her face has gone all stony and closed. It's over now." But her chair was empty. She knelt next to him, elbowing the waitress aside.

Liz took charge of the situation, starting by telling the

waitress, who now scurried around their table spouting apologies and self-criticism, to get some wet cloths. Gary felt a delicate plucking at his collar. "I got this shrimp before it could go down your shirt," Liz informed him. "And let me just . . . ." A strange scraping sensation tickled the small of his back. "There. Hey, iced tea spoons are perfect for flipping soggy fries out of a guy's pants. I think you can stand up now." She pulled him to his feet, nodding sympathetically as the sauce and grease soaked shirt slid unpleasantly across his skin.

The waitress came back with damp handtowels, and Liz scraped more sauce and food from his shoulders and back. "Y'all's meals will be on the house," the waitress said anxiously, with a hopeful smile.

"I don't think I'm hungry anymore," Gary groaned.

Liz worked quickly, clearing the main clumps of food from his clothes right away so that they could stop providing a spectacle for the other customers to observe. They moved to the foyer, where she wiped him down more thoroughly. Gary thought that some men would extract arousal from the sensation of Liz's long fingers moving from shoulder to waist, but he wasn't that sort. He did take note, however, of the fact that her hair had come loose here and there, stray wisps drifting at the sides. She dropped the savory towels on the floor next to a gumball machine and sized him up. "You don't look bad from the front, except for the breading and mayonnaise in your hair."

In the trunk of his car, Gary found an old piece of newspaper to spread out on the driver's seat. He unlocked the door for Liz, then hesitated. "I think I have to take this shirt off," he told her, and she just shrugged.

"Nothing I haven't seen before."

Gary balled up the shirt inside out and tossed it into the trunk, briefly struck a muscle-man pose, then climbed in and fired up the engine. They roared up old Highway 51 between two walls of sunstruck jungle, the force of their passage ruffling the shirts of the men who sat with cane poles just off the road, jerking cat-fish up out of the canal. Liz and Gary discussed the seafood fi-asco from every angle. He invited her to tune the radio as she saw fit, and soon the smooth sounds of the Bee Gees, Peter Cetera, Carole King, and the rest of the gang filled the car, courtesy of WFLT-AM. Gary detoured through Hammond, and they picked up barbecue sandwiches from Hi-Ho, which they both declared tasted better than fried seafood anyway. The high point of the day came when she poked her fingers into her bun and pulled out a hair pin. It was not quite the librarian-turns-out-to-be-sexy mo-ment of unimaginative movies, since she spent two minutes plucking pin after pin from her hair and had no glasses to cast aside, but gradually her hair fell loose and Gary went a little breathless at the sight of her. She opened the top button of her dress. "Sometimes I wonder," she sighed.

"Yeah." He hoped he understood her correctly. Would this be the time to bring up the I-20 rest stop and the large pur-ple tour bus?

They had just crossed the Lexington Parish line when Liz suddenly spoke up. "So what did you think of the service?" she asked, lowering the volume on "I Write the Songs."

He drummed his fingers along the top rim of the steer-ing wheel, hoping a diplomatic answer might occur to him. "The service?" The truth was that he could not help wondering whether he should throw her in the trunk and take her down to his apartment on Magazine Street, where he could duct tape her to the couch and keep her captive for a few days--weeks? How-ever long it would take her to see the folly of the Creepers and admit that it would be better to live a regular life, perhaps at-tending a more established church, one whose name had been a registered trademark for centuries: Methodist, Episcopalian, even Baptist. Instead of answering, he asked a question. "Why are they called the Creepers?"

"We really don't call ourselves the Creepers, but you probably noticed that we don't believe in speaking the name of Cripes out loud, and instead we use other names, like Jeepers Creepers, names which originally arose as a way of stifling the impulse to take the Lord's name in vain. That's all. It's not like we believe in sneaking around on all fours to show our devotion to Criminy." The late afternoon shadows of skinny Lexington Parish pines flashed across her face, giving her a strange, intermittent radiance. "Did you enjoy the service?" She hurriedly tucked her hair behind her ears.

"It was really interesting," Gary admitted, guiding the car onto the long road that would bring them back to her church, where she had left her car. He speculated that there might be specialists who guided people like her out of the darkness, perhaps by swinging a pocket watch, speaking quietly, and snapping their fingers dramatically. What would it take to get her into some sort of rehab center, where she could take group therapy with recovering Moonies and Swaggartians? "But why can't you use His name? What's wrong with saying it?"

She smiled as if she had expected his question and spoke as if she had answered it many times in her life. "His name is the most sacred thing we have. Daily usage would make it seem mundane, even meaningless."

What would happen if I took her to one of Minister Hayes' services? Gary wondered. Where would she end up after having her senses assaulted by the name of Jesus for one solid hour? He worried that it would drive her insane, or send her back to the Creepers even more certain that theirs was the right way. "But isn't there any time when it's appropriate?" he asked.

She took a hairpin from the console and began re-bunning. "Only when addressing Him directly."

"But your preacher prayed to Gosh," he pointed out.

"Praying isn't addressing Him directly. You would have to be face to face."

"But isn't Golly all around us?" he asked, gesturing toward the woods.

"Gosh rules in heaven," she said, picking up more pins. "This world is but a vapor."

"It is?" The car burst through a sunlit clearing, grass and weeds replacing the pines.

"Of course it is." She studied the last pin for a moment, then poked it deep into her bun. "Turn here."

Gary braked hard and swerved into the grassy lot next to her church. He watched her cast a grave look toward the white building, then pull down the visor and carefully check her bun, turning this way and that before the mirror. The sapphire dress lent a glow to her delicate throat, and he couldn't help wondering if kissing her and telling her how much he adored her awkward beauty might convince her to come away from the church.

She turned toward him, smiling. "Would you like to come again next Sunday?"

"Uh," Gary said. "Um, well, I think-- I don't think I'll be able to."

"Okay," she said cheerily, but there was a steely undertone she couldn't disguise. "Well, today was a lot of fun." She began to open the door.

"Maybe we can try Manchac again soon," he called. "I'll wear protective clothing."

"Thanks for the ride," she called as the door shut, then strode to her car without looking back.

Over the next ten days, Gary thought of her often. He wandered his barren apartment at night, picking lint off the furniture and reviewing every moment of their Sunday together. Some days he pictured her laughing, hair down, singing Paul Anka tunes; other days he could only picture the back of her head as she walked away. Standing at a railing by the river watching a seemingly uninhabited freighter slide by, he wondered if she might call him, realizing that he had never gotten her number. Suddenly New Orleans seemed like the perfect place for solitude, for mooning about gazing at freighters. It was easy to go to a dingy cafe late at night and sit by the window drinking coffee while the lone waitress chewed her gum and waited for other lonely customers to show up. He found a spacious bar on the edge of the Quarter where no one else wanted to shoot pool in the middle of a Tuesday afternoon, and he stayed there for hours playing blues and country on the jukebox, unable to decide which sounded more forlorn. Every time he took a walk around his neighborhood it rained, and he always wound up strolling slowly down the middle of a deserted street with his jacket slung over one shoulder. At such times he tried to whistle mournful tunes, though he never did find the echoey acoustics to suit his mood. The culmination came on the day he had a flat tire and had to take a bus to work. On the way home, the bus took a long, un-expected detour, during which the other passengers gradually dis-appeared. It began to rain, hard enough that the water streamed steadily down the window. Gary leaned his head against the glass, eyeing the city wearily. The bus stopped at a red light, and he sat staring into a cemetery crowded with whitewashed mausoleums. I'll be lonely in the afterlife too, won't I? he thought, then won-dered if he would have an afterlife, heathen that he was-- neither a Proclaimer nor a Creeper.

Desperate, unable to bear his empty rooms and the dis-appointing phone calls from young men in distant states who wanted him to buy pet insurance, Gary left work early one day and lit out for Lexington Parish. He drove fast, trying not to cook up any sort of plan, though he toyed with the idea of waltzing into the Creepers' church and leaving Liz a note, operating on the assumption that she always sat in the same spot on the same pew. But what would he write? He told himself to stop thinking about it, that he was going home to be around people he knew. Those empty country roads were not nearly as lonesome as the city streets had been lately-- if you waited just a few minutes any time of day, a pickup truck was sure to come along, and the driver was sure to lift a hand in greeting.

He came roaring into the outskirts on Highway 190, still maintaining expressway speed. In the middle distance he spotted a faded plywood sign in the shape of an ice cream cone, and in the spirit of not having a plan he slowed, veering into the lot of the drive-through. There was nothing to it but the crude sign, a shell-paved lot, two decrepit picnic tables, and a low cinderblock building with a walk-up window, but it had been the place to go for cones, burgers, and succulent po-boys for as long as he could remember. Just before he pulled in between two Chevy extra-cabs, he caught sight of her standing behind three boys at the walk-up window. Was that really her? he wondered, unable to see around the truck now that he had parked. It was and it wasn't: her hair, but more loosely fixed-- not exactly a ponytail and not exactly a bun. Her rather jagged profile, smoothed by wraparound tortoiseshell shades. And she wore a skirt, one that hugged her legs and ended just above the knee. A sister?

"Gary," she called as he came toward the window, still checking the parking lot for her mother's forbidding Crown Vic.

"It is you," he said happily.

"I thought about calling," she confessed.

"I thought about kidnapping you and taking you down to Grand Isle for a picnic on the beach," he laughed, caught on a giddy wave.

She gave him the answer of his dreams. "How about to-morrow?"

"I can abduct you at ten."

She scribbled directions to her apartment in Ponchatoula as they ate their soft-serve at one of the picnic tables. They parted in high spirits, and Gary sped back to New Orleans with a sense of accomplishment.

When he got home, there was a message from Liz. She sounded much more serious and cautious than she had been at the drive-through. "Gary. It's Liz. Just wanted to let you know that I have Bible study at the church tomorrow at five-thirty, so I can't stay in Grand Isle for too long. Also, uh, I wanted you to understand that I won't be swimming tomorrow, since we don't believe in bathing suits." He knew what "we" meant, and it dampened his spirits a little, though he summoned the energy to stay up late packing the ice chest with the most elaborate picnic foods he could assemble from his meagerly stocked refrigerator.

"So, do you own a bathing suit?" Gary asked as they drove down narrow Highway 1, the land around them gradually becoming more and more perforated by canals, bayous, and bays.

Liz put on a glossy, unreadable smile of the sort beauty-pageant contestants wear. "I do have one, although I never did until a few years ago. Once in a while I might swim with a tee shirt over it, though not in mixed company. Hey, how about some oldies?" She lunged for the radio the way marathon runners lunge for cups of water.

Who needs the big city? Gary thought, even as he joked and sang with Liz. Who needs a high salary, a slick coupe? Who needs pork in hot garlic sauce at a bustling world-class restaurant filled with men wearing dark suits? Who needs to sleep unnaturally late on Sundays and watch football in pajamas? Who needs an office on the seventeenth floor of a copper-hued glass building? Who needs to flirt with women who shellac their hair and color their lips and pluck their eyebrows? There were so many better things to be had, like piney woods and that drive-through fried chicken and two-lane roads and Saturday fish fries and simple wooden benches and genuine whitewash and modest clothes and sermons and hymns which used Gosh and Cripes to talk about God and Christ, and a person could probably get used to that, couldn't he? And wasn't that much better than not going to church at all, better than having only embarrassing memories and an unappeasable longing?

A Carpenters song came on as the car climbed the high bridge that would deliver them to Grand Isle. From the crest of the rise, the Gulf below appeared to nearly swallow the narrow strip of land. Liz sat forward at the sight of it, sighed. "I had forgotten how it looked," she said. "I used to go to my uncle's camp, and he would take us fishing. I guess we never went to the beach." When she settled back in her seat again, she seemed to be positioned closer to him. "Isn't it nice to come down here like this, no reason to hurry, good music, good company?" She smiled warmly at him, so warmly that Gary let the car wander onto the shoulder for a moment.

"You're right," he said, waiting for her to loosen her hair. He slowed the car as they came into town. From ground level the earth seemed solid enough, though there were dunes and stilted houses lining both sides of the road. A few minutes later he handed a few dollars to the ranger manning the entrance of the state park and drove in. After parking, he stared at the steering wheel for a moment.

"Is this the beach you usually come to?" Liz asked, and opened her door.

They pulled the ice chest and blanket from the trunk. She stooped and helpfully grasped one of the ice-chest handles when he appeared ready. Threading their way between sea oats, they crested the dunes. The Gulf pulsated gently before them, casting long, low waves that rustled against the sand. The water ran flat to the horizon, etched by light ripples. Liz dropped her end of the ice chest. "This is lovely," she said, and gaped at the water, the long expanse of uneven sand, the bulky line of piled-up seaweed, the crooked dunes and waving grasses. "I never realized."

"They say it eases the mind to look at water."

"It does!" she declared, and wandered around to his side, still gaping. "Look at the colors!" The next thing Gary knew, she had turned from the Gulf to him, pulling him off-balance with a clumsy embrace. Then she was running down off the dune. "Look!" She waded through a heap of seaweed, stirring it with her bare feet and stooping to lift a strand.

By the time he had kicked off his sandals and joined her, she was at the water's edge. The low waves washed her feet and licked at the hem of her skirt. "It feels warm," she marveled.

"I thought you'd like it." He splashed a little water toward her.

"I have to just…. " She looked up and down the beach furtively, then took two handfuls of her skirt and lifted slightly. She kept lifting as Gary waded out with her until the water reached their knees. They looked at each other for a long moment, and Gary pined for her more desperately than ever. If only one of us were a little different, he thought. Then Liz yanked the skirt up and over her head, revealing the bottom half of a modest maroon swimsuit. "Will you hold this?" She handed Gary the balled up skirt.

She moved to deeper water, saying, "Oh my God! I can't believe I'm doing this!" As she paused to pull off her blouse and toss it back to him, part of him wanted to shout, "Don't do it!" The rest of him yelled, popped champagne, and lit firecrackers.

Gang of Three

In a flash I perceived that the light blue shorts and deceptively whimsical white truck were accessories to his disguise. Every mechanism of his subterfuge lay exposed in that moment as I watched him trudge off across the lawn toward the next house, mailbag bouncing at his hip with insincere cheerfulness.

I realized that he was not the innocuous mailman I had taken him for. He had the smooth, neatly groomed, physically fit look that I associated with a certain species of writer-- the annoyingly successful, those who make it look easy. He no doubt had some sensitive, literary name such as David (not Dave) or Gilbert. Oh, how David/Gilbert must have gloated when in my mail he had first spotted the telltale manila envelope with its return address from *Jackass Review* or *Cantaloupe Quarterly*, so heavy with returned manuscript, so rejection-laden. And how his eyes must have narrowed as he had pocketed the white business envelope, hand addressed, that had carried my acceptance letter from *Prose Journal* or *The Quotidian*. He had the look of one who would do anything to eliminate the competition. What other explanation could there be for my long dry spell?

The mailbag no doubt had many hidden compartments for such purloinings. And I felt that the fury of my vision could rip the bag to shreds as Gilbert/David trundled on toward Mr. Purdy's house, toward Mr. Purdy himself, who had as usual found an excuse to emerge from his shadowy doorway just before the mail arrived. I heard Purdy begin to jabber at Gilbert, though I was not close enough to make out the words. Not that I could make out actual words when speaking to Purdy face-to-face. Gilbert feigned comprehension, nodding over-emphatically as he handed him his mail, then hiked off to the next house. I darted back inside before Purdy could notice my presence and wave me over to hear another of his incoherent commentaries, and I sat down just in time to catch the Doppler Gang's noon forecast.

It was the allure of the Doppler Gang that drew me daily from the laborious forging of crooked sentence upon crooked sentence in my unkempt study. With their help, I had begun to understand the differences between partly sunny and partly cloudy. I treasured equally old Ted's sober take on flash flood watches and ozone readings, Lily's enthusiasm for tide ranges, and Sparky's ready acknowledgement of his junior position. I often threw down the pen a little early and caught the whole newscast, so great was my anticipation. Occasionally I even allowed myself to view the preceding game/talk show, *Couples Therapy*. I reassured myself that there was no harm in curtailing my writing for the sake of television. Curtailing? I felt that I was simply stopping, it being time to stop, since I had been at it for almost more than roughly an hour. I reasoned that the secluding aspect of the writing process, the holing-up-in-a-garret-away-from-society side of it, must be balanced by a certain sociability, a turning-on-the-tube-to-stay-up-on-things mentality.

A similar theory had led me to introduce myself to Mr. Purdy the previous year, soon after Gwen and I moved in. Fetching the paper one partly cloudy morning with a thirty percent chance of rain, I noticed that the white-haired old man I had seen through the blinds was kneeling in his driveway, poking dispiritedly at a row of tulips. Fighting the urge to hustle back to the sanctuary of my house, I crossed the yard to approach this neighbor, even though as I came closer I saw that his mouth was a slack hole in a field of white stubble. I was glad to see the mouth close as he moved spryly to his feet. "Hello, I'm James Schooner!" I announced cheerfully.

The man waved his trowel toward me, toward my house, and said something about having seen me move in, or so I gathered. He seemed to say, "Yeah I seen a truck a bad other day got rye up in a straw day."

"Yes sir!" I replied, smile freezing, and I spent the next quarter hour repeating that mantra, sometimes tossing in a hearty "I see!" for good measure. The man spoke quickly, sloppily, and loudly. I surmised that we were discussing gardens, women, and weather, though it was difficult to tell. At one point the trowel hung loosely in his hand, drooping toward the tulips as he said something about how pretty they were, and I realized that a strong country accent further distorted my neighbor's speech. I tried not to enunciate too correctively as I turned to the flowers and said, "Yes, they are pretty." It was not until a week later, an hour after Mrs. Hatcher across the street said she had seen me talking to Mr. Purdy, that I understood my neighbor had not been describing the tulips, but had been telling me his name. I felt the heat of a searing retroactive blush.

If not for Mr. Purdy, I may have had more success following Gilbert through the neighborhood. In the days following my intuitive discovery of Gilbert's deceptions, the image of his blue-clad form came to haunt me, pressing itself insistently into my thoughts after the lights were off. It wasn't just that limber, tanned hand casually working the white envelope into an obscure pocket of the mailbag, that heavy-lidded smirk. I also imagined Gilbert seated at an antique wooden table illuminated by a small cone of light, leather-bound tomes lining the walls, black coffee steaming in a flowery porcelain cup as he wielded some sort of tortoiseshell fountain pen on taupe parchment, his words flowing evenly and rapidly across the page, blackening the paper with tales of vivid green apples and concrete towers, a man writhing in the fire of self-imposed trouble, the low thrum of another's assurances breaking the silence of an evening. I remembered when I had been able to write like that, when my first book had come pouring out, and when it had been no struggle to find a publisher. I had thought my novel would be the first in a long string of successes, and I danced in my kitchen on the day it hit the shelves. I cheerfully dismissed the fact that no one seemed to notice my book there on those shelves-- not readers, buyers, critics, editors, librarians, or agents. When my second was ignored immediately after I had finished it, never even reaching the shelves, I ruefully but confidently chalked it up to experience and began working on another. By the time I had discovered Gilbert's ruse, six years had passed and even small press journals showed no interest in my writing. I tried not to wonder if I would one day stop writing and become altogether incoherent, an old ghost like Mr. Purdy. The opus I imagined Gilbert writing resembled my own first efforts-- pure, elemental, universal. In that sense it was more like *Beowulf* itself than my current project, a contemporary retelling of the epic, in which I rendered the hero as a photocopier repairman named Bob Wulf.

I made my attempt to follow Gilbert along his route in part because I was having such trouble getting past the banquet scene of *Bob Wulf*. It had been easy to compose the opening, in which, rather than being sighted by the Danes from the cliffs as his ship approaches, the hero is noticed by a paralegal on the second floor as he pulls up in his minivan. My pen, with its cumbersome load of unwritten words, grew clumsier in section two, where Bob joins a sumptuous pastry banquet in the coffee room and hears woeful tales of paper jams and spewing toner. Suddenly I could hardly think of the next sentence, and each day it became more and more difficult to stay at my desk, especially with the chiming clock signaling the fact that my host, Dr. Jimmy Victoria, would soon jog onto the set of *Couples Therapy* to introduce the day's patient-contestants. I also listened for the clank of the mailbox lid, convinced that the editors of the *Whitebread Review* had had enough time to read my latest short story and determine its publication date.

A week or so after I saw through Gilbert's deceit, on a partly sunny day with winds shifting to the northwest by mid-afternoon, I heard the clank just as Dr. Jimmy penalized couple number two for rationalizing their tendency to alienate convenience-store clerks. I bolted from my chair and traveled to the door in two quick bounds. Having spent the last ten minutes at my desk calculating the number of days it had taken my manuscript to travel up to Vermont and how many days my story had languished in the *Whitebread Review* slush pile (with careful consideration given to the number of assistant editors named on their masthead), I was especially anxious for the mail. I had given the associate editor and editor-in-chief a generous five days each and allowed four days for the letter of acceptance to travel back from Vermont. I seized upon the fact that it was the best story I had ever written and upon the fact that the *Whitebread Review* had recently published a story that was clearly inferior to my own efforts, and I concluded that acceptance was guaranteed. You can imagine the plummeting disappointment I felt upon opening the brass box to discover nothing but a "Have You Seen Me?" ad for beltless slacks.

"Bastard," I muttered, not sure whether I was slandering Gilbert, myself, or the middle-aged Ken doll modeling pants in the advertisement. By the time I had fetched my keys and trotted out into the front yard, Gilbert was two houses down, moving through the spotty shadows of a stately live oak. I set out after him, staying commando-low and going from tree to tree. Before I had gone far, I came across Mr. Purdy, who wore a more bewildered expression than usual, possibly because he was sitting down on and among his yellow tulips. I halted before him, frustration welling as I watched Gilbert's uniformed figure dwindle into the distance.

"Did Gilbert do this?" I demanded.

"Who?" Purdy hooted.

"The mailman— did he push you or something?" I leaned over and took his upper arm, finding it shockingly thin, then levered him up to an unsteady stance.

"Nah," Mr. Purdy scoffed. "Got these flowers attend to, yeah sure to pull tea weed a bit." He gave the seat of his pants a few hearty slaps and staggered toward the screen door.

"Someone's been tossing bottles into your flower beds," I called after him. The screen door slammed itself.

I plucked two empty half-pints of Johnny Daniels whiskey from his tulips, then shuffled stiffly back to my own house, feeling rather old— not as old as Purdy, but certainly not as young as Gilbert, either. It was easy to picture Gilbert striding effortlessly through the soft air, moving from house to house with his ever lighter bag of mail, speed increasing with each delivery, stride lengthening from stroll to jog, then to a steady run, sneakered feet pounding surely over lawn, concrete, asphalt, legs folding abruptly to hurdle low fences and garden gnomes. And the experiences! To come across the ambulance idling in the driveway, to witness the collisions of automobiles in the street, the collisions of lives before living room windows; to be the one to rescue fallen baby birds and squirrels, to catch a child's ball before it careens into the path of an errant eighteen-wheeler full of copiers and counter parts. Only when I looked about and realized that I now slouched on my sofa, ignoring the Doppler Gang in favor of an absurd fantasy in which Gilbert climbed a tree for a worried old lady and came down cradling her kitten— only then did I slap my own cheek to knock myself out of the reverie.

My trip to the health club a few days later was a similar attempt to jolt my sluggish spirit. We were under the influence of a dome of high pressure, and it was one of those clear, dry days, rain chance zero percent, that brought out a special cheeriness in the Doppler Gang, even Ted. Despite the inspiring meteorological conditions, I had been unable to concentrate on Bob Wulf all morning, though I stubbornly sat at my desk staring at the blank half of the page while my mind spun further tales of Gilbert's doings. I had begun to fear that his misdeeds went beyond merely pilfering acceptance letters and returned manuscripts. Perhaps the *Whitebread Review* had actually rejected my story of a modern incarnation of Robinson Crusoe (Robbie Suncruiser, locked in a bedding factory overnight). Unlikely as that seemed, it raised the possibility that my manuscript now lay atop Gilbert's stack of *National Geographics*, and that soon Gilbert would read the story out of boredom of a Wednesday evening and, recognizing its brilliance, would scan the entire piece into the slim laptop lying open on his antique wooden desk. Next it was a simple matter of changing the name and address on the first page, perhaps making a few stylistic alterations in keeping with his preference for coordinate adjectives and occasional fragments. And then there was Nina, Associate Editor Nina. On the rejection notice for my previous story ("Dick Moby"), she had taken the time to write, "Thanks, James. I am sorry we can't use this." I couldn't help but read a certain affection into her composition of the note. I pictured the way she had flicked three fingers through her tresses as she decided that "Thanks, James" sounded so much more intimate than "James: Thank you," or worse yet, "Dear Mr. Schooner." I was sure the use of "I" in place of the usual editorial "we" was significant too, because she wanted me to know that she felt a little wistful, that if it were up to her alone . . . that she loved the story, and knew from its gentle, subtle conclusion that

I was someone she desired to know better. I had begun the cover letter for my next submission ("Robbie Suncruiser") with the words "Dear Nina," and had meant them sincerely, hoping she could sense my return of her affection. For all I knew, Nina's rejection of "Robbie Suncruiser," now in Gilbert's possession, was softened by a postscript revealing that she would be in town on business soon and would love to meet with me. She was surely beautiful, or at least pretty, and well-connected. And if a meeting were arranged, she would meet not me but handsome, athletic Gilbert. I could only hope that she might realize a week into the romance that Gilbert was too immature to have written the sublime "Robbie Suncruiser."

Gilbert's edge, though, the edge which might allow him to close the maturity gap between us, was that he was out there every day, interacting with Purdy, handing an orange kitten to old Mrs. Pope, murmuring with the concerned residents of South River Oaks as paramedics hustled a loaded stretcher across some poor soul's yard. All I ever did was sleep, eat, write, watch television, read, go to my lonely job as night proofreader for a local textbook company, and exchange a few sporadic words with Gwen as we brushed our teeth or drank coffee. I knew it was important for writers to mingle and interact with the world at large, and that I had neglected to do so for too long. After I mustered the energy to pack a gym bag and step through the door, going to the health club was not so difficult. Before I had even left the locker room, I was glad I had come. The heady smell of sweat, sour shoes, and the fumes of cologne, deodorant, and hairspray energized me. This was the real thing. We men were naked, half-naked, sweaty, hairy, jostling one another.

A few moments later I walked through a room of stationary unicycles and into the bright echoes of the natatorium. The man swimming in lane three immediately caught my attention with his white swimsuit. It was small and rather tight, and I laughed because it reminded me of briefs, as if the man had made a mistake in the locker room. The wearer of the white suit was churning along in a fast crawl, and as he turned his face for a gasp of air I caught sight of Gilbert's strong brow and black hair. Or was it someone else? I knew how water could distort hair color, and he moved away quickly. I followed him, shuffling along the side of the pool, acting as if I were looking for an empty chair on which to leave my towel, but keeping my gaze fixed on the elusive face of the swimmer in white. After four steps my foot struck a chair, crushing my toe. Fighting to suppress a grimace, I limped after the swimmer, hoping to get a better view without entering his field of vision. Long, muscular legs, short hair— dark, if not black— and something postal in the way he swam, with the same steady, determined pace that carried him through my neighborhood. The man was in the last quarter of his lap now, and I had an inspired thought: I would casually pass along the end of the pool just as he made his turn, so that I might see his face more clearly. I had to hurry, and I thumped along one-legged, raising my arms to slip between the wall and an old man in a wetsuit. I looked down just as Gilbert surfaced, blowing and huffing before submerging again to kick off from the tiles, shooting away underwater. The caginess around the eyes and the crafty curl of his lip left no doubt that it was Gilbert. I was not sure he had seen me and hoped that he had not, for I had been wearing a rather ovine, surprised expression, my hands still halfway raised as if I held a harpoon at the ready.

When Gilbert hauled himself out of the other end of the pool a few moments later and grabbed a towel as he strolled back toward the locker room, I drifted after him at some distance. It was as if I were tied to him by a lengthy rope. I loitered within view of the door to the showers until he emerged, then learned that our lockers were three rows apart, which helped me remain inconspicuous, but made him difficult to track. Still wrapped in a towel, I hurried to a toilet stall to blow my nose unnecessarily, noting as I passed that Gilbert had pulled on shorts and was busy unrolling his socks. A few minutes later, barefoot, I passed him in my hastily donned slacks and shirt on my way to the sink for a superfluous hand-wash; Gilbert was shod and dressed, though his hair was messy and his shirt unbuttoned. I panicked and rushed back to my locker for my shoes and bag, and in a few seconds I was all ready to go, but when I casually drifted down the aisle, Gilbert was gone. His locker remained open, and I soon spotted him standing in front of a mirror. For ten minutes he spritzed his hair, deodorized his armpits, cologned his face, and lotioned his chest and arms.

I had no particular plan but still felt that an invisible cable attached me to him. As he walked out of the health club, I thought I would just see what he drove and leave it at that, but when he pulled out of the parking lot and headed west, I followed. The rope between us was elastic enough that I did not feel compelled to tailgate, but allowed cars and even one red light to separate us. Nevertheless, when I momentarily lost sight of him on a curve, I found myself speeding up and passing a slow Honda rather aggressively. Gilbert piloted a fairly ancient Mazda, no doubt part of his elaborate facade— just as no one would think the postman was a successful writer, few would look twice at the driver of such a ragged vehicle.

When he darted into the parking lot of Dark Mirror Coffeehouse, I nearly shot past him, but managed to careen to the right and shoot into a space a good distance from where he had parked. I just caught sight of him passing through the coffeehouse door as I put the transmission in park. Well, this has gone far enough, I thought, and tried to tell myself to put the car in reverse and go home. Instead I sat there with the engine running, staring at the door of Dark Mirror and struggling to resist the tug of the line connecting us. It seemed too great a risk to be in the same small space with Gilbert, where there would be nothing to hide behind. Then again, with the baseball cap I dug out of the back seat and the sunglasses I wore to drive, I was almost incognito.

I had some trouble finding Gilbert in the dim coffeehouse, looking through those dark glasses. Not to be conspicuous, I went right up to the counter and ordered a semi-large decaf pumpkin cream latte with whole milk to go. I took a long sip, hiding behind the cup as I turned from the counter and surveyed the room. Gilbert sat by the window at a small table, talking to a woman with freckles and curly blond hair. I came close to choking on my sweet latte, for I was sure that I was witnessing the first meeting between Associate Editor Nina and a dastardly impostor.

I picked up a stray newspaper and sat in the corner to observe. She had that gentle, literary look, the look of one who has an intuitive grasp of good sentence structure and an ear for poetry, the look of one who would be wearing a heather gray cable-knit sweater if it were not such a hot day. She wore wire-rim glasses— smart, stylish ones. She smiled at Gilbert warmly, nodded at what he was saying— all the time thinking he was me. The latte wasn't hot enough, and I wished it were as bitter as coal.

It took a long time. Gilbert had a large iced tea and was sucking it down fairly quickly, while I conserved my latte, but I had neglected to visit the restroom at the health club because of my preoccupation with Gilbert. It was touch and go for a while there, but he finally stood up and made a vague gesture toward the men's room. As soon as he moved out of sight, I jumped up and raced to their table, taking Gilbert's seat. "Hi," I said to Nina. I thought she was even more beautiful up close, where I could see just how fine and smooth her skin was.

"Hi?" She shifted uncomfortably, checked over her shoulder for Gilbert's return.

"He's pretending to be someone else," I murmured.

"Who?"

"Him. I mean, me. He's pretending to be me."

"He is?"

"Look, he knows about 'Robbie Suncruiser' but ask him about 'Dick Moby,' okay?"

"Don't you mean Moby Dick? What is this about, anyway? Are you a buddy of his?"

It wasn't so much her ignorance of "Dick Moby" as her choice of words. No self-respecting Associate Editor would say "buddy" for "friend," even in casual conversation. This person, whoever she was, might be semi-smart and fairly beautiful, but she was certainly no Nina. I managed to choke out a weak "Never mind" before I bolted, leaving my half-empty cup on their table.

By the following overcast day with highs in the high eighties, lows in the low sixties, I had developed the theory that the false Nina I had spoken to was postal herself, a colleague of Gilbert's if not a cohort. It seemed quite feasible that she was even a writer like him. I briefly theorized that she might even be a co-conspirator, sabotaging another struggling writer on her own route, but concluded that I was not quite so poor a judge of character. Her literary quality had caught my eye first, but with much late-night consideration I saw that there was a deliberate, trudging quality to her bearing as well. The whole episode made me all the more anxious to hear from the real Nina, whose acceptance/love letter was a week overdue by this point, and I made sure I was installed within earshot of the mailbox well before Gilbert's usual delivery time.

Despite the fact that the Doppler Gang was in mid-forecast, offering cheerful warnings of dangerous afternoon hail, I vaulted up from the couch the moment I heard the brass lid slam shut. The sight of a large manila envelope protruding from the box sucked all of the air out of my chest, and I swayed a little, eyes closed, praying that this was merely a rejection of the admittedly clumsy "Pictures of Dory and Gray," a recent submission to the *Yellow Mustard Quarterly*. The exterior offered no clues, as there was no return address and, as sometimes happened, no postmark canceling the stamps I had applied. Only my own address, scrawled in my own hand. I shot a wary glance toward Gilbert's receding back and tore the envelope open, finding my story, my "Robbie Suncruiser," and a small printed card: *It grieves us to inform you that the enclosed item does not meet our editorial needs at this time, despite its great beauty, intrinsic excellence, and many innovative features. We are eternally grateful that you considered the* Whitebread Review, *and hope that your item will win awards and widespread admiration elsewhere in the extremely near future. The Editors.*

"That does it," I muttered, experiencing a new moment of clarity, one that pierced the deepest layers of Gilbert's trickery. Instead of gleefully steaming uncanceled stamps off of return envelopes that came back with no postmarks, I should have been getting on the phone with the postmaster, contacting lawyers and private investigators. It had been so easy, and he was so smug. He probably considered himself a genius, had probably laughed when he had decided what to do with the outgoing manuscripts I sometimes left in my brass mailbox, as I had done with "Robbie Suncruiser." It was not enough to read them and throw them away. Now he was packing up the return envelope a few weeks after the theft, then hand delivering it back to me with the rejection note from one of his own pitiful stories slipped inside.

"Hey!" I shouted, launching myself from the porch and chugging off after Gilbert, who was still visible two houses down. I felt gigantic, inspired; in a surge I sensed every detail of my next story, "The Strange Case of James Jekyll and Gilbert Hyde." Gilbert gave no sign of having heard me, but I imagined the panic he would feel at knowing the jig was up. "Hold on there!" I bellowed. His head swiveled as if he had heard a distant sound.

lowed. His head swiveled as if he had heard a distant sound. "Hey!" I yelled again, from the middle of Mr. Purdy's yard. He turned around. "Yes, you," I said.

"What's going on?" he called, then did a strange thing. He dropped his mailbag and ran toward me full tilt. I ground to a halt on Mr. Purdy's lawn, blanching at the prospect of the impending tackle and scuffle. For a moment everything was much worse than I had imagined.

But Gilbert veered off at the other end of Mr. Purdy's yard and disappeared behind the high azalea bushes that obscured the front of the house. He reappeared for a moment, waving frantically to me. "Come on, man!" he yelled. "The guy looks dead!"

I sprinted clumsily around the azaleas to find Gilbert kneeling beside Mr. Purdy, who lay in the grass on his back, legs awkwardly arranged, eyes closed, mouth open. I stopped, reached for Purdy's shoulder. Gilbert knocked my hand aside with his forearm. "Don't touch him!" he said. "You don't never disturb a crime scene."

"What did you say?" Our eyes met. I saw none of the caginess I believed I had detected from a distance. His eyelids were actually a little droopy.

"Looks to me like someone knocked him on the head, or maybe he just keeled plumb over."

"Right." I would have rolled my eyes if I hadn't felt so stupid for having imagined Gilbert— or whatever his name was— to be a writer. "Mr. Purdy," I said loudly, taking note of the half-pint of Johnny Daniels that lay under the nearest azalea. "Are you all right, sir? Can you hear me?"

Mr. Purdy opened gray-blue eyes that seemed to mirror the pewter sky. He snorted in amusement, propped himself up on his elbows. "Looks like the windmill won this round. Which one of you would be Sancho Panza?" he asked crisply, looking at

Gilbert, then at me.

Gilbert made a face and shrugged, met my gaze. "He don't make no sense," he whispered. Mr. Purdy promptly offered one hand to me, and I hauled him to his feet, gingerly brushing the grass and leaves from his back. As we moved arm-in-arm toward Mr. Purdy's front door and Gilbert trotted back to his mailbag, ice pellets the size of pencil erasers began to fall from the clouds.

Guttering Out

She showed up at the wrong time. Although Curtis thought she was beautiful the moment he saw her, wondered what she was like, felt a thrill when she came toward him, and wanted to whoop and jump when she started dancing with and smiling at him, he soon stopped paying attention. They had hardly danced two minutes when "The Wreck of the Edgar Fitzpatrick" came on, and the song led his mind away from the girl with the two-tone hair and the well-worn jeans that would hold the shape of her body for hours after being removed.

He could not have said when the sidetracking had begun, though it was certainly after the whole crackup back home in Toledo, and had gotten worse the further he had wandered and the more he had slept on sidewalks. In Louisville one night he had stopped running from a baseball-bat-wielding convenience store manager because as he passed an appliance store the television in the window showed a purple-clad football player fumbling a handoff. Suddenly, knowing whether the player recovered the ball mattered more than escaping the wrath of his pursuer. Later on, in Memphis, he had trouble concentrating on his friends' hand signals and whispered jokes as they waited out an evening rain in the public library, because he kept hearing snatches of a children's story being read down the hall. Finally he had muttered something about finding the bathroom and searched out the story-teller, mainly to make sure the little penguin found its misplaced eggs. By the end of the story, his friends were gone. He wasn't sure where they would be sleeping that night, and the easiest solution was to walk out onto the interstate on-ramp and start hitching again.

The girl smiled as she danced, kicking out her elbows and bouncing happily. In the pause before someone put on "The Wreck of the Edgar Fitzpatrick," she stumbled against him playfully. "You been to Bill's parties before?" she asked.

"I don't even . . . ." Curtis made a hand gesture that he hoped told her how the older guy whom he guessed might have been Bill had called out to Rudy when they were all down behind the French Market, telling them to come to the party at his apartment on Esplanade.

"Bill loves everybody," she said fondly, but Curtis hardly heard her, galvanized as he was by the opening lines of "The Wreck of the Edgar Fitzpatrick." "Well, the seas were real high and the wind howled low as they loaded the Edgar Fitzpatrick," sang a luminous voice. Curtis swayed slightly as he listened, rapt. The girl kept smiling for a while and swayed along with the slow music too, but Curtis wasn't dancing. The tale drew him in, and he vividly imagined the steady captain on the pitching bridge, the frantic crew in the engine room, the roaring waves, the looming rocks, and every other image the mournful lyrics sketched. He hadn't noticed the gradual evacuation of the dance floor as the song droned nasally on and on, because to him it was no nasal drone— it was lustrous, penetrating, poignant music, imbued with a majesty absent from the usual Primus and Filter CDs he used to have. By the time the ship lost steerage and began drifting toward the rocks, Curtis was crouched beside the nearest speaker, hoping for a miraculous Coast Guard rescue in the next verse. The girl was nowhere to be seen. Not that he looked for her.

He had another chance the next day. He found Rudy and

Sky and Bernice and the others sitting on a stone curb among the milling tourists in Jackson Square, close enough to the obese fortune teller's table to laugh at the deranged advice he gave his customers. "Don't use a power saw for the next couple of months," he told a lady with white hair, patting her hand.

"Here comes that new chick," Cooper said, watching Curtis' dance partner approach, black and vanilla hair vivid in the sun.

"Jan's not new," Rudy scoffed. "You're new. She was here before I was."

"Move that fine thing over," Jan told Curtis as she sat down, bumping his hip with hers. She had a black cat tattooed on her upper arm, and the skin behind it was pale and soft, nothing like his own taut, reddish arm.

"Do you stay . . . ?" He pointed across the square, made a hand arc indicating the Y, the sidewalks along Decatur, the Moonwalk, and all of the other places they sat and talked and ate and slept.

"I sleep at my sister's sometimes," she confessed. "But she just moved uptown. So, yeah, around here mostly."

"Yeah," Curtis said, and they regarded each other for a moment. A flash of intuition or desire gave him glimpses of hiking in the desert, riding bicycles, getting into a car, chopping onions beside her.

Curtis' curiosity killed the moment with Jan when a fluty voice nearby asked, "Where can he be?" He turned toward the voice and found its source: a fresh-scrubbed young woman in white shorts passing in front of the fortune teller's table.

"We have to find him," whined one of a trio of children beside her, casting fragile glances up toward a man with glasses and a buzz cut.

"Can't turn your back for a second," the dad groused, his words fading into the background of music and voices filling the square. Now Jan was leaning across Curtis' lap to joke with Sky about having her over for a barbecue if she promised to wear a corsage. He hardly heard or felt her. The family of tourists turned a corner and disappeared, but he kept his eyes on the last place he had seen them, praying they would return.

"Come on, blue eyes," Jan called. Curtis was surprised to see her and the others ten yards off, mostly with their backs to him. He hurried to join them, but paid little attention to where they were going. Thoughts of those children occupied his mind.

He imagined how they must have sung and chanted and passed books back and forth all through the long drive down from Tulsa, getting mean and crying once in a while, marveling at every cheap restaurant and motel, at the novelty of being in a swimming pool at ten p.m. And now alternating between boredom and exhilaration in a strange city— museum, riverboat, department store, aquarium. And the unsettling smell of raw sewage or rank garbage that haunted certain side streets, the incomprehensible sight of pierced, tattooed, unwashed big kids asking for change or lying comfortably across the sidewalk, a sight Curtis would have found puzzling back when he thought divorce was for other people and had never imagined that his brother could drown in a quarry and lie pale in a blue-cushioned casket. And now what? He wondered if those children's baby brother had toppled into the treacherous river when no one was looking, or if their father had gone off on a casino-and-vodka binge and the buzz-cut guy was just an uncle. The whole mystery gave Curtis the jitters, made it hard for him to concentrate on what happened around him. He hardly noticed Jan beside him on the way to the plaza, where they all sat on the rim of a fountain, hoping to run into some skaters, guys with money and cars and parents, who might stop slamming their boards around long enough to talk a while, maybe pass a joint or take them on a beer run with a stop at the McDonald's drive-through. Jan talked to Curtis and he talked to her, but he didn't follow what she said very closely. Something about wishing she could move to San Francisco, live in a big old boarding house near Haight-Ashbury, work at a funky bookstore.

The others took more note than he did of the fact that she stayed near him all day. They sat on the sidewalk out in front of a funky dress shop on Decatur, and as usual Curtis sat at the end, but Jan placed herself next to him so that he was not the very tail of their uneven line, and she goaded him into speculating about which pedestrians had screwed each other the night before. They all spread out along the Moonwalk in the late afternoon, collecting change from the tourists who came to gawk at the Mississippi, and Jan paired herself with Curtis, which suited him since it meant he had little to do except smile hopefully when Jan said, "We're kind of stranded. Do you think you could spare a little change?" When she held his hand, he assumed it was to make the "we" more convincing.

After they finished, Jan and Curtis sat on a bench to watch freighters and barges grind their way up and down the river. She started to mention that her dad had once said life was a river, to muse that it was more like a department store, to tell him something about Chicago, a lumberyard, a young teacher, shoplifting, a sleeping bag. But the woman on the next bench over was telling her son a story that intrigued Curtis much more, because Jan's wasn't really a story. "He was drunk, of course," the woman was saying. To Curtis she was obviously a retired school teacher, probably from Oregon or Pennsylvania, and her son was maybe a mechanic who had trouble holding a job but she liked it that way and had nothing else to do, so here they were on vacation in New Orleans. "Dancing around in front of the window with some sort of scarf. This was on the seventh floor, mind you. He's dancing, trying to spin in a funny way but of course he's drunk. So, guess what? Boom. He trips, he falls against the glass, it breaks, he tumbles on out and goes down, down, down seven stories. Aaaaaaaah! Maybe it was eight stories. I forget. Anyway, he hits the ground, smack, right into the mud puddle, a big mud puddle there in the garden or whatever. They rush to the window, they scream, the men run downstairs, they call 911, the whole bit. Meanwhile, he sits up, looks around, starts wiping the mud off. 'What happened?' he asks. So they take him to the hospital for X-rays and all, and he's perfectly fine. Not a scratch on him. Can you believe that?"

"Wow," Curtis said.

"I know," Jan laughed. "But I wonder if things would work out in Frisco, or would I want to be back in New Orleans? It's a little scary."

What happens next? Curtis wondered. No one ever explains what happens after the story ends. The ship wrecks, the team wins, the man survives his fall, the penguin finds the eggs, the brother drowns, but then what? What do people do next? Do they become parts of other stories, and if so, how long do they wait before the next one starts?

She kissed him in an alleyway off Chartres. The air had gone soft with the dropping of the sun, and chimney swifts darted and chattered high above the rooftops. Suddenly she guided him between two buildings, grinning and kicking garbage bags aside. Her mouth felt compact, delicate, lively, and one cool hand dug into his pants. "I have some money saved from temping," she breathed, laughing. "I was thinking of really going out west. You could come too, Curtis."

"Where?" he wanted to ask, but before he could do so he heard an incredible thing. "I hope there's no line," said a familiar, fluty voice. "I hate waiting."

"I'll think about it," he told Jan, giving her enough of a smile to excuse his sidling back out to the sidewalk. "Let's catch up with the others." Jan tightened her lips and lowered her brow, though Curtis failed to notice.

It looked like the kids would get to stay up past their bedtime, because the whole tourist family was there, scuttling up the stretch of sidewalk between Curtis and his friends, who had stopped at the next corner. Curtis quickened his stride, came close enough to hear the family's conversation. "It wasn't so much the food as the price," the dad commented.

"We'll try to eat cheap tomorrow," Mom promised.

"I can just eat peanut butter and jelly," one of the children offered helpfully.

Where is the baby that fell in the river? Curtis wondered, because they were not talking as if they had just lost one. He could tell by the way the children trotted happily to keep up with their parents that everything had turned out all right. As they neared the corner where Rudy and the others loitered, Dad guided them into the street to avoid the menacing group. Curtis knew that if he didn't follow them he would never sleep, and he studied the family again, thinking perhaps one of them pushed an inconspicuous stroller. Finally he saw the stuffed yellow Space Toddler tucked under the arm of the little boy who had whined so desperately that morning. Curtis pictured the Space Toddler lying forlorn under a restaurant chair, imagined its despair turning to joy when at last the boy had found it. That's all there was to it. One lost toy.

Curtis and Jan stood with Rudy and Sky and the others for a while. Nobody seemed willing to say which way they should go next. They yawned, watched tourists amble past, gazed up and down the street. Jan finally broke away from the group, taking reluctant steps toward Canal Street. "Where you going?" Sky called.

"Bus station," Jan replied. Curtis heard her but didn't know what it meant.

It was a Tuesday night, too close to fall for there to be much going on, even on Bourbon Street. Rudy figured sitting on the sidewalk near a row of strip bars might be worth a try. They could always watch the tourists strolling unawares into the sleazy part of Bourbon, some of them hooting and laughing, others putting their heads down and hurrying through. And in a couple of hours most of the passersby would be drunk, and there would be cigarettes to bum, change to collect, maybe even swigs to take.

But Bourbon was sparsely peopled, mostly by locals who knew how to ignore Curtis and Rudy and the others. Curtis grew drowsy and slouched lower, not caring how far his legs extended across the sidewalk. Cooper's bulky shoulder made a suitable cushion for the side of his head. His eyes closed, and the sounds of the street and of his friends talking flickered off, then on. A ship blew its horn out on the river. "Did you see what happened?" a voice asked.

"You mean those two?" said another.

"She's got a crush on him this big, and he don't even know it."

"So why's she taking off now?"

Curtis' mind roused itself, though his eyes stayed shut. He wondered who spoke, and if the subject of their gossip was nearby. Could be those two bouncers from across the way, talking about the red-haired stripper and some slick banker, or a couple of college students from Indiana walking ten paces behind their friends. He wriggled into a more upright position, looked around. "Jan must think he's not—" Sky began, but Rudy shushed her and nodded toward Curtis. "Have a good nap?" Sky asked innocently.

Feeling like a sailor on the pitching deck of a Great Lakes freighter who sees a Coast Guard chopper cutting through the rain, Curtis read the gist of the past day or so and sensed the outline of the next chapter. He blinked at Sky and Rudy. "Too long," he said, and struggled to his feet. "Which way is the bus station?"

The Story of Jane and George

One hot cloudy Saturday late in July, George pulled his old Honda onto a patch of gravel alongside River Road and set the hand brake. The levee, rising up in front of him and his wife, looked like any other small steep hill, if you ignored the length of it. It faded into the distance in either direction, and he imagined it snaking all the way south to the Gulf, all the way north into the woods of Minnesota. It had never occurred to him that there could be much of anything lying beyond something so bare and simple.

He looked at his wife. "Here we are," he said, trying to remember her name. She gave him a pure smile that dizzied him, and leaned toward him. She kissed his cheek and said "Thank you" in his ear. That was what she said when she didn't know what else to say, and George knew that in this case it meant she was happy to be there with him. He was happy, too—the sight of her delicate cheekbones and glittering black eyes poured giddiness into the marrow of his bones.

When he opened his door and stepped out of the car onto the gravel, she did the same on her side. He'd once told her to stay put and let him come around to open the door, but she'd pretended not to understand. She knew far more English than he knew Vietnamese—his Vietnamese vocabulary had to do with beer, food, weapons, commands, and sex. Her understanding was usually very fluent, even if her accent was thick, but occasionally there were gaps in her comprehension at convenient times. When he had asked her how she pronounced her real name, for example, she had shrugged and just pointed to it, there on her immigration papers. "But how do you say it?" he had asked her, and she had showed it to him again. He had wanted to ask again, but they were in a crowd at the city clerk's office, waiting to get their marriage license. That had been in Galveston, in March, which seemed like years ago and thousands of miles away. All he could remember now, in Baton Rouge, was that her name had p's and n's in it, and o's and u's. The adopted name he knew her by was Jane.

The two of them hardly spoke as George pushed open a small wooden gate in the pasture fence and as they began to climb the mown slope of the levee. They rarely spoke very much anyway. He was pretty sure that the strength of their love allowed them to communicate without words. He knew when she didn't mind just sitting and thinking or watching TV, and when she wanted to be entertained or taken somewhere. He knew how close to hold her, and she knew when he was depressed and edgy and shouldn't be disturbed. He had sensed, earlier that afternoon, that she didn't want to just sit next to him while he watched an Astros game.

"What would you like to do?" he'd said, turning the game off at the end of the fourth inning, pretending it was over already.

"Oh I dunno Joy." She'd shrugged. She called him Joy most of the time, except in bed, where she more slowly and carefully formed every letter of his name.

"You haven't seen the Mississippi River yet," he said. "Neither have I, not really."

"No, I haven't," she'd said, shrugging again. George and Jane had crossed the big river bridge into Baton Rouge one night six weeks before, making the move from Galveston. The little car had strained to pull the rented trailer up the slope of the long steel span, but at the top every weight had seemed to lift from the car and from George's chest. The river twinkled blackly, his wife slept lightly beside him, and they descended into a new city at high speed.

Things had gotten rough on both of them in Galveston before they were married. George had felt the beginnings of a subtle persecution when he started to appear with Jane in public. In the mall, in the grocery store, even just driving down the street he had felt stared at, talked about, laughed at meanly. He could tell that similar things were happening to Jane. "Don't you know her?" he'd asked her when they saw a plump Vietnamese woman in the meat department of the Piggly Wiggly near the waterfront. "I don't know her," Jane had said, not looking. When she and the woman spoke briefly in the cereal aisle, he thought their words sounded harsh and unfriendly. "What did she say?" he asked as they moved on toward paper products. "She say, 'Hello, how are you?'" Jane had answered.

But he knew it was worth it—every unspoken confrontation was worth the trouble. At home at night without Jane, he would look back over the time they'd spent together with satisfaction. We'll fight them all our lives if we have to, he'd think defiantly. His determination grew out of a feeling he'd had the very minute he'd met her. He'd noticed a little hair salon on a side street near his office. "Hair cutting—men and women," the tiny sign had read. The first time he'd seen the salon, it had been empty despite the lunch-hour rush that flowed by a few feet from the door. He made a mental note, thinking it was probably cheap and there'd be no wait.

The following Tuesday, he'd gone into the little shop after a quick lunch nearby. It was empty, but at last a stocky little man came out. "Please," he'd said, pointing to one of the two barber chairs. He disappeared into the back room again.

George leaned back in the chair, thinking maybe the man was Italian, but he could be Indian or Latin. He'd closed his eyes and soon heard light footsteps behind him. Gentle hands wrapped a paper collar around his neck, and fastened the plastic sheet over it. George looked at the smudged toe of his left wingtip. "How you like hair?" a musical voice had asked. She turned him to face the mirror. A round-faced Asian woman with her hair pulled back in a broad ponytail, gold rings in her ears, stood just behind him. George blinked. "How should I cut?" she'd asked after another moment. "Just a trim. No sideburns," he'd said at last.

As she snipped, he found out things he'd been almost sure of the moment he saw her: she was indeed from Viet Nam. She had lived through the war. She was beautiful. He was infatuated. Yes, she would let him take her to a movie. And he'd marveled: I once fought in her country, against her people. But barriers are down now; love makes no distinctions. It doesn't matter where we were born, what we've seen, only that we are a man and a woman, drawn together. That feeling had stayed with him for a long time, through all of the difficulties in Galveston.

After two months of marriage and several months of waging a silent battle against the community, George had casually mentioned the fact that his firm needed someone to help set up a Baton Rouge office. Jane had looked down at her plate and said, just as casually, "You going to do it?" He had nodded, knowing that she wanted him to, and that a change—any change—would do them good. He'd longed to be where no one knew them.

As George climbed the levee hillside, the thousand girders of the river bridge came into view. He stopped, let Jane catch up. "See?" he pointed. "There's that bridge. You were asleep."

"I see," she said, and kept climbing. He watched her small feet wobbling a little on her wedge heels as she climbed in front of him. The tops of trees came into view above the crest of the levee, to his surprise. He had expected to find a simple slope down to a simple large river, on the other side of the levee. Instead he found a shell road along the top and another pasture inclining down toward a narrow strip of still, greenish water, surrounded by mossy trees and brush. A thin hump of weedy dirt cut through the trees and water to a steep shore of broken concrete blocks, weeds, and trash. Beyond it all flowed the dull brown river, a half mile wide.

"You ever see a river this big?" he asked her, as she stood beside him on the shells, gazing out at the strange panorama before them.

"Many times," she replied, and started down the other side of the hill.

George began to follow. He didn't know much of what Jane had seen in Viet Nam, although she knew all about what he had seen there. One of the things they did talk about at length was George's war experience, although their talks weren't quite conversations. They were more like monologues, and they happened mostly in the mornings, just after both of them woke up, especially on weekends, when they would lie late in bed. Sometimes a bad dream he'd had would prompt him. Usually he kept talking, sending his words up to the quiet white ceiling, because he sensed that it was somehow therapeutic. So he'd lie there with a hand behind his head and a hand on Jane's hip, telling her about things like the time Dennis Balogh was killed by a frail-looking old man with a wooden knife, or about the feeling he'd get on long treks through wet dark jungles: that the fabric of his uniform was grafting itself to his skin, melded by sweat, mold and water; and that the canteen, the gun, the helmet—all the hard things—were sinking into him, joining themselves to his skeleton. It seemed then that he would be a soldier in the woods forever.

She always listened silently, sometimes adding tender strokes. George sensed that she knew it was good for him, that she knew he had to say these things aloud. It lifted his spirits to think that he had someone who understood him so intuitively.

As they crossed the little land bridge over the stagnant ponds by the river, Jane's hat blew off her head. It was a black broad-brimmed hat she'd bought during their first week in Baton Rouge. George had never told her how good he thought it looked, but he loved it on her, and she wore it often as though she knew. It landed flat on the surface of the ugly water and floated there, moving not at all. The river breeze that had taken it seemed not to reach the low water.

"My hat! Joy, look!" she cried, putting her hands on her hips and staring angrily at her hat.

George squinted at the water, wondering how deep it might be. It was too covered in leaves and algae to tell. He caught a whiff of its dank vegetable smell.

"It's all right," she said, but he knew it was not all right. She wanted her hat back.

He kicked his way through the weeds on the little steep bank. Just as his foot slipped on the mud and splashed into the water, he thought of stopping to remove his shoes and socks and to roll up his pants. The water was only inches deep there at the edge, but it felt uncannily warm on his ankle, and for some reason he was glad he'd kept his shoes on.

"I'll get it," he told Jane.

"Careful," she said quietly. The hat was sitting right in the center of the pond. The top of the brim was dry—it sat on the flat water as if it were on a table. He waded further, slowly. He was sweating in the oppressive heat. Cicadas screamed in the trees at an unreal volume. The thick brush, the mossy trees, the water, the heat, his own cautious motions: I know where I am, George thought. This is Louisiana, he told himself, Louisiana, Louisiana, Louisiana, with every step. The water deepened to his knee, then in a sudden drop down, to his waist.

Just as he got to the point where he thought he could lean out and reach the hat—when he'd started to lean, ready to snatch the hat and thrash ashore—something heavy and dark rose up on the other side of the pond, not ten yards away. It was grey, tall, sudden. It raised its arms. George found his heart stopping, found one hand reaching for the place where he had carried his knife, the other trying to unsling a rifle from his shoulder. He slipped backwards, finding himself under dark water, the light of the sky disappearing.

He thrashed his way to the land bridge, to Jane. She waited with her arms open, stooping to pull him out of the water. "Shit, oh shit," he sputtered. His heart still felt too large in his chest.

"Look. Look, Joy," Jane pointed out over the river. A grey heron was working its way slowly up through the air, away from them. "It scared you, huh?" she said.

"Yeah. Terrified," he said. I need to sit down, he thought. What a nightmare.

Jane smiled at him, touched his shoulder. "That's funny, Joy. One big bird scare you." She laughed. "And my hat sank."

Very funny, George thought. It could have killed me. But he got the idea that Jane was laughing because she believed it might be healthy for him, therapeutic.

George slept without dreaming that night, and the next morning, Sunday, he and Jane lay in bed with breakfast and the newspaper. At first they spoke only to offer one another more coffee or more toast and to ask for sections of the paper. Both were content, it seemed. He had no desire to narrate any old war stories and somehow knew she probably didn't want to hear any.

The closest he came to mentioning the war was after he put the sports section aside and leaned back into the pillows, gazing out through the screens at the sun-soaked sweet olive tree, at grackles hopping back and forth in the upper branches. He thought of his encounter with the heron and smiled to himself. I feel better, he thought, almost as if he might be able to forget the war now—the sudden scare acting like a shock treatment. He had to let Jane know what he was feeling. "That thing with the heron yesterday," he said with a little laugh. She nodded without looking up from the book reviews. "I feel better now. You know what I was thinking when that bird flew up?"

She stopped reading and stared at him. Her mind seemed far away. "Yes, I know," she said.

Of course she knew—that's what was so great. George leaned forward eagerly. "But it's like I'm cured now. I could—"

"No," Jane said quickly. "You're not cured now. You can't." She went back to reading. George shrugged. She'd see.

After they had finished the paper, they showered together, dressed together, and ate ham sandwiches on the back porch of their little blue house. After lunch, George sat down in front of another Astros game. Jane went out to the garden and stayed out there for four and two-thirds innings. She came in out of the sun and sat down next to him, curled her feet up under herself and leaned against him on the couch. She smelled of black soil and perfume. He put his arm around her and kept watching the game. She looked at her nails for a minute, pulling dirt out from under them. She looked at George's nails, one by one. She shifted, straightening up and crossing her legs. She ate three of his potato chips, and when a first baseman came to bat, she laughed and said, "That man is fat."

When the fifth inning was over, George got up and turned the TV off. He stretched. "Good game?" Jane asked.

He nodded. "You want to go see something?" he said casually.

"Sure, Joy, if you want." Jane shrugged, then got up and went back toward the bedroom. He knew she'd look in the mirror, touch her hair, get a scarf from the closet and be out with her shoes on in less than a minute. George tucked his shirt in, sighing and smiling. This was all so simple, so easy and good.

He looked at a map before they left and drove them to a section of the city bordering the river that was expanded on the map and labeled "Downtown Baton Rouge." The area seemed almost deserted though, with streets too wide for the trickle of traffic and a lot of stores that looked to be closed for good. Right near the river there was a sign saying "Catfish Town." They drove past a long brick building, a mystifying sign that said "USSKIDD," and a small chain of antique railroad cars. All of this was new to them, and all of it seemed to be uninhabited. George parked on a side street directly across from the passenger cars. He and Jane got out of the car and walked slowly across the broad four-lane street. He did his best to absorb every detail: the gold-painted numbers on the green bodies of the Pullmans, the slow breeze coming down the street, and the deep drone of engines pushing barges up the Mississippi. So this is it, he told himself. This is where we live now, where we'll live happily. Moving away from Galveston was all it took.

He held Jane's hand as they approached the railroad cars. Stairs led up into the nearest one, and the door looked open, but with no one around George didn't feel like they should investigate. They walked on, along the front of the brick building. A sign by the front door said "LASC Museum." He halted and peered through the door, but it looked closed or empty, and there was nothing of interest anywhere in sight.

Just beyond the museum, the levee was paved and terraced into stairways, landings, little plazas with fountains. As George led Jane up the stairs to investigate, he looked toward the river and was startled to see the grey metal stacks and rods of the top of a warship, poking up over the levee. "Oh, the U.S.S. *Kidd* is a ship," he said aloud.

"What, Joy?" Jane said, tugging at his hand.

"The U.S.S. *Kidd* is a ship. I thought the sign said 'Usskidd' before," he said.

"So?"

"It's a ship. I think I've heard of it before. Have I? Where did I hear that name?"

"I never hear of it," Jane said. She shrugged. "There's nothing here to see."

He began to walk toward the ship, pulling Jane along. "Was it my dad, or Alan?" he said.

"Alan?"

"My brother in St. Louis."

"Oh, him," Jane said. She slowed her pace, falling a step behind him but still holding his hand tightly. "We should maybe go somewhere better, Joy."

George's father had been in the Navy in World War II, and his oldest brother Alan had been in the Navy during and after the Korean war. George, the baby of eight children but only the second son, had broken with family tradition by being in the Army, and by waiting until he was drafted instead of signing up at the first hint of trouble. Sometimes he talked to Jane about how disappointed his father had been in him and in the whole Viet Nam thing until just a few years ago. Several times, during his morning monologues, George had lamented to Jane "the tragic tradition of war in the Fletcher family." Saying such things, dramatic things, always made him feel so much better.

He and Jane came to a broad paved walkway over the river, and stood looking down on a smallish warship (a destroyer? George wondered) bristling with funnels, ladders, antennae, and big guns. There was a little ticket booth down there, and a long gangplank leading up onto the ship. The *Kidd* looked well maintained; to George it looked majestic, awesome, American. It cut a sharp figure, with its cannons and high prow. His eyes glistened.

Jane's eyes glistened too, until they began to overflow.

George turned to say "Let's go" and lead her down to the ship, but he found her turning away, raising her free hand and trying to hide her wet cheeks. It cut his heart deeply. He knew he had done the wrong thing, had been doing the wrong thing for some time now. He had an urge to pound his own head or fall to his knees, to find some way to punish himself. "What...?" he said. Jane shook her head and took a step back. He knew she wanted him to take her home, to drive her to their house and take her inside, take care of her.

The rest of the afternoon, Jane worked quietly in the garden, insisting that she was all right, that she wanted to. George sat in a lawn chair in the shade of the house, watching her and wondering what exactly had scared her so much.

Was it the guns? The thought of narrow metal passages, tiny doors? The thought of walking down to the ticket booth and seeing the brutal hull towering over her? She had never told how she came from Viet Nam to the United States, though he knew she'd arrived in 1978. Anything could have happened on the expanse of water between their countries.

That night George couldn't get to sleep. The room was filled with the watery yellow light of a near-full moon and the hushed call of hundreds of crickets. He turned from his side to his back to his stomach to his other side, to no avail. Jane lay still, on her back, but he sensed that she was awake, listening to his sighs. He told himself to think good thoughts and found himself remembering the way things had been when he and Jane first met. She'd been living with a brother and three cousins in a tiny apartment near the waterfront, and their only problems had involved mild cultural conflicts. He thought of the time he'd come to pick her up and she wasn't quite ready. He'd sat in the little living room, among strange food smells and strange decorations, listening to three Vietnamese men argue in the kitchen. He had felt so foreign, but that was only a discomfort. It was easy enough to leave with Jane and feel at home again. That may have been the night they went straight to George's apartment, the night he realized how comfortable she was with him and he with her—how at home they were. Nationalities and memories had still faded away at the lightest touch; it was easy to believe that all were brothers, all were sisters. Not any more, George thought, shifting to lie on his back again. Now there seemed to be a painful gulf between them.

As the clock crept toward two, he turned to her and carefully laid his arm across her waist. "You need to talk, Joy?" she whispered.

"No." He moved closer. "I want you to talk," he said carefully.

She rolled away from him, sitting up and putting her feet to the floor. Fragilely, she rose. He watched her, alarmed by the way her long filmy gown made her look like a weightless ghost. His heart quickened. "Where are you going?" he asked in a hoarse voice.

"A glass of water," she murmured, moving off toward the bathroom. She stopped, now nearly hidden in shadow. "Then I come back and tell you some things."

She came back after five minutes of running the water. He wasn't sure in the dim light, but it looked like she was gliding through the room with her eyes closed. She shooed him aside and sat on his edge of the bed. George put one hand on her leg and curled around her, lying on his side. She palmed his cheek gently, her hand cold and damp. "There are too many things," she said quietly.

George waited. They stayed like that for minutes. "Things?" he said at last.

She nodded. "How long did you visit?"

"Visit?"

"To my country."

"About a year." He began to guess what she would say next.

"I was born in there. Twenty five years. It went worse and worse—French war, your war, Viet Cong winning. Terrible mess."

"I know."

"You still fix things from one year. I have more to fix."

"You have to start," he whispered.

"I will start, but—" She paused. "You don't cure them, not even one year."

"No," he admitted. The moon rose higher and higher as she began to tell him some of the things she'd gone through, and its light grew brighter and bluer. He didn't have to ask questions. Instead he took a cue from her and moved his hand slowly against her skin while she spoke alone. He listened, absorbing, startled again and again by sudden flushes of understanding and the embarrassment of never having bothered to ask what had happened. He bit his tongue to keep from apologizing. The gradual death of her family—younger sisters to rocket fire, her uncle to prison when the war was over, a brother to the communist army, who disappeared in the invasion of Cambodia. Her mother never coming back from market one day. An aunt her age who spent all her money on passage aboard an aging fishing boat. She'd disappeared too. "No letters. No way to know. Pirates, storms, gun boats. It makes me cry." All of it came flooding out of her, disaster after disaster. She spoke evenly, not crying or frowning or pausing.

Once she laughed a little. "The river you so proud of? Can you swim over it?"

"No," George said mystified.

"The Mekong was bigger, Joy." She smiled.

"You swam it?"

She nodded proudly. "You didn't take a boat like your aunt?" he asked, ashamed that he didn't know.

"My father and brother said we would walk over Cambodia to Thailand. We heard of pirates." For a long time she described the journey, and George was silent again. The treacherous guides. Checkpoints where she had to separate from her brother and father and hope no one addressed her in Khmer, hope the sarong and the dirt she'd rubbed into her fair complexion made her look like a native. The day the Viet Cong had stopped her father and she'd had to walk past like an unconcerned farmer. She and her brother had crept slowly closer to Thailand, dodging Khmer Rouge and Viet Cong soldiers and the Para, who controlled the jungles. "They all had guns," she said. "All very angry. Violent for everyone." She paused, and George sensed a great bulk of trouble behind what she was saying, things she was leaving out for now.

She went on for almost two hours. She described the refugee camps near the Thai border. "No water. Terrible smells and no spaces. Everybody was at the end of tragedy," she said. "Going crazy." The delirious hope they pinned on the Red Cross workers, the nightly raids by Para soldiers, the shooting and shelling that drew too close at times. "The trip was a year," she told him. "Me and my brother were alone," she added, and stopped.

George wanted to gasp for breath. He felt as if he' d been held under water for too long, but it wasn't him—she was the one who'd been blasted by torrents, thrashed and shaken. Just hearing about it had half drowned him. She must be so strong, he thought. Enormously strong.

She climbed over him and lay in the middle of the bed, pulling herself close against his back. She groaned. "I'll tell more tomorrow," she said sleepily.

"Plenty of time," he said, and felt her nod. Deliriously relieved, he began to drowse, his breathing matching hers, but a last question came to him. "How do you say your name?" he asked.

He heard only her steady breathing. After that he dropped off, anxious for morning.

That German Girl

You'd better not fall in love, she said, the morning after a beautiful Italian girl knocked on our bedroom door during an intimate 3 a.m. moment.

She'd gone to the door to see what the beautiful Italian girl needed. I lay in bed stiffly, hoping that if the beautiful Italian girl got a glimpse of me in the imperfect darkness of the bedroom when the door opened, she'd think nothing of me, that I'd look asleep or at least sleepy. I heard rapid, urgent whispering, some "I'm sorry, so sorry" and some "Okay, okay, let's see…."

Suspense may be adequately defined by the experience of lying awake at three, wondering why a beautiful Italian girl has come to your door while you were making love to your wife. On a school night.

It's not that I didn't know why the Italian girl was sleeping under our roof. Her presence was no surprise, but her knocking had startled us, almost to a panic. "What could she want?" Kate had asked. "Are we being loud?"

Before bed, we had made sure the beautiful Italian girl had everything she needed: towel, toothbrush, pillowcase, a place to put her shoes, and the knowledge that she could help herself to anything in the kitchen.

Possibilities ran through my mind. A prowler—perhaps some perverse neighbor who had noted the arrival of a beautiful Italian girl with a large suitcase in the middle of the afternoon—

had come to her window. Perhaps she could not find any toilet paper. The dog had pooped on her bed?

"I think she's having a panic attack," Kate whispered upon her return to bed. "She was freaked out, couldn't sleep. It's no wonder, with all she's been through."

The beautiful Italian girl had washed up on our doorstep after the storm. For her the storm had lasted for two weeks. She spent the week before landfall packing up and leaving her hometown in Italy, flying across the Atlantic, finding her way around New Orleans and Loyola University, moving in and buying books and getting ready for an American year of grad school. Then one of her roommates walked into her bedroom and said, "We're leaving! A storm is coming! Bring your suitcase!" A week of sloshing around the southeast followed: long hours in hot cars, disoriented hurrying, snatches of television news, long distance phone calls. Somehow she found out that LSU would admit her while Loyola recovered from the flood. Baton Rouge was crowded with sick, traumatized evacuees, but after a few emails and a phone call or two, she stood in our living room with one hand on the giant blue suitcase she'd dragged behind her through the whole ordeal. "Down, Kiki," Kate said to the dog, and then introduced our daughter Gina to the beautiful Italian girl.

Lying in another new bed, still not at home but having found a place to stay, she must have found the silence after the storm deafening. The bewildered mind that had had to be decisive and resourceful for so long now had to stop short, but it couldn't. It kept revving and surging, in search of solutions that had already been found. The heart would not slow, but instead gathered more and more momentum as the walls of our spare bedroom leaned in closer.

The next morning, I made pancakes while Kate sat at the breakfast table showing the beautiful Italian girl a map of the city. Gina waved to the Italian girl and made eyes at her until she felt comfortable enough to climb up into her lap. "You can take the bus to the university on Monday," Kate said. "Or maybe I'll drive you over there for the first few days." Gina wrapped her arms around the beautiful Italian girl's neck and squeezed too hard.

There are so many other stories I could be telling, like the one about the time I happened on Ross and his cohorts jimmying Pontiac locks just as the attendant came along and blew fuel at them through a tube, or the one about the community getting into an uproar over my student's newly revealed homosexuality, which led to my saying, "The ACLU'll be all over you, rug-boy!" to his toupeed landlord.

I did not fall in love with the beautiful Italian girl, though I certainly could have, had I let myself. She was smart, tall and curvy, with thick sexy hair and a thick sexy accent. "Someone needs to take her to get her books tonight," Kate said on Sunday. I shrugged calmly, said I wasn't busy. "Maybe I should take her, though," she concluded, and that is what she did.

The storm had come in like a giant egg-beater and just scrambled the whole Gulf coast. It wrecked the city Kate and I used to live in and killed two thousand people. Its floodwaters carried away my friend Lizzie's cats and rabbits, though I like to think they clung to an old fencepost that drifted past, riding a benevolent current out to Lake Pontchartrain, through the Rigolets and on to the Gulf, ending up feral on their own sandy island. It trapped my friend Mary in her house for two days, until a boat came and took her to a highway overpass, where she baked in the sun for four more days waiting for help. It brought beautiful Italian girls to the houses of unsuspecting married couples, then moved inland, fizzling out without telling anyone what to do about the mess it had left behind.

I feel a little like the people I sat with at breakfast in Arizona three months after 9/11. Once everyone had served themselves and exchanged enough pleasantries that everyone knew who everyone else was, there came a lull as we all wondered what to talk about. Someone mentioned Harry Potter, and we were off and running. Adults—forty, fifty, sixty-year-olds—talking at length about Harry Potter, instead of talking about that other thing, that thing that still made us feel sick to our stomachs, that thing we had already talked about for three months.

Did I mention the time I helped a friend look for relics in a house he had bought where Elvis had once filmed a practice movie, finding a nice boom box and some cameras with undeveloped film? Or the time we were all joking about the snake-proof garbage bags Mama had bought? The next time I took the trash out, a big copperhead came out of the neighbor's long grass and tried to *git* me. No? Not interested?

"My God, she's adventurous," Kate told me in bed on Sunday night. She had driven the beautiful Italian girl to the university bookstore after dinner, been gone two hours. I can't recall exactly what Kate told me, but it had to do with backpacking around Europe, up to the furthest reaches of Finland, sleeping in hostels, on beaches, and in the apartments of people she met along the way. "She went two weeks without a shower one time," Kate said. I knew that even with chapped lips, greasy hair pulled back in a rough ponytail, arms brown from sun and dirt, a grimy pack on her back, she was still beautiful.

Has your imagination ever pounded on a door in the back of your head when you know it's towing a whole crate full of grainy photos of a different head lying on the pillow next to yours and a different body taking off and putting on clothes or just walking beside you, and tapes of another voice whispering and laughing and calling to you? If you're strong enough, you change the subject, start wondering whether you can spare the money for tinted windows and alloy wheels and how much longer you can go without mowing the lawn. Maybe that's not so much strength as love.

Kate drove her over to the university in the morning. "Maybe you can pick her up after work," she told me on the phone around lunch time, but she ended up being the one to go get her while I put some dinner together. The two of them came in right around the time I took the potatoes out of the oven, both of them laughing, both beautiful.

I might as well tell you that Kate will be crying by the end of this story. Unless you'd rather hear about the student whose car I once borrowed. As I slid behind the wheel, she showed me a lump of crack the size and shape of a large potato she kept beneath the seat. After much thought, I pocketed it on my way to St. Francisville and placed a scolding note in its niche under the driver's seat, although the thought of dealer vengeance led me to discard the note and replace the crack tater. Weird, huh?

"We stopped for coffee," Kate explained later. "Do you know she went to India with her fiance last year, and they broke up halfway through the trip? She wandered all over India for six months on her own." I didn't need to hear that, considering the text of the Kama Sutra I'd uploaded to my brain back in college, whose imaginary illustrations had always featured me and Kate, not me and the beautiful Italian girl. I worked on wondering whether one of the Olsen twins was anorexic and who our next governor would be.

I pulled some sweatpants on before I left the bedroom to brush my teeth that night. The beautiful Italian girl was just coming out of the bathroom when I came out into the hall. "Hi," I said, with a shrug. She gave me a sweet smile and said "Hi." I'd be lying if I said I didn't notice the lace edging the neck of her cotton nightgown, or if I said that's all I noticed.

"You should take her out to Alligator Bayou," Kate said one night. "She loves nature, wildlife, things like that." We debated the merits of Saturday versus Sunday, morning versus afternoon. "It's too bad you can't go," I said dutifully. "Oh, I trust you," she joked.

So early Saturday morning I put two kayaks, one red and one yellow, on top of the truck and stowed paddles and lifejackets in the back. The beautiful Italian girl came out of the house wearing a pair of Kate's khaki shorts just as I tightened the last strap. Those shorts were a little looser on her and had taken on a somewhat cuter shape, if you must know.

I've been thinking about the time when (years ago) I caught sight of a young woman crossing the backyard at a party. She had an elegant nose, purple lipstick, and a black beret. "She must be that German girl the others were talking about," I thought, and the next time she passed by I trotted out my high school deutsch: *"Guten abend,"* I said, and got the funniest look. "What did you say?" she asked. Kate always liked that story.

The dirt road out to Alligator Bayou had survived the storm, barely, and the boat launch was not exactly open, but the guys shoring up the bait shop and clearing off downed trees said it was okay. I managed to help the beautiful Italian girl into the red kayak without touching her, then shoved the boat out into the flat, dark water. She paddled away capably as I scrambled into the yellow kayak and pushed back.

The narrow bayou winds away from the boat launch, cutting through wild hardwood forest. The kayaks tore black slits in the flat green surface, pushing aside a thin layer of floating duckweed. The beautiful Italian girl could not stop smiling. "So wonderful," she said. "Thank you for bringing me." A kingfisher fussed at us, then flew off along the surface.

We came around a bend and both saw a big truck tire lying in the shallows 100 yards ahead. We went "tsk-tsk" and shook our heads. "Why should somebody disturb this beauty?" she said.

When we got closer, I could see that the dark thing was not a truck tire. "Oh, it's a dead gator," I said. "What a shame."

"Did someone hunt him?" she asked.

"Sometimes hunters or fishermen take potshots," I said, shrugging. "It's a huge one, too."

I would not have kissed her if the alligator had not come to life and chased after us, if it had not been so huge, if I had realized sooner what had really happened. But I'm getting ahead of myself. Let me back up. Did you know that when Kate and I were in England, she closed her finger in the door getting out of a cab? We got right back in the cab and asked the driver to take us to the emergency room, confusing him further by asking if he had any band-aids in the glove compartment. No, he said. "Any plasters in the glove box?" I asked, and when he opened it a whole slew of bandages cascaded out. But I may have gone back too far there. I should say that the beautiful Italian girl and I glided cautiously up to the gator's carcass, curious and silent. We came close enough to see that its head and tail were submerged, the knobby treads of its curved back exposed above the water. Why isn't it belly-up? I wondered, looking for gunshot wounds. "Ooh," the beautiful Italian girl cooed piteously. I nodded, back-paddling softly to avoid poking the gator with the point of my boat, at which point it came to life. Vigorously to life. It thrashed one way, its heavy body making a C, then the other way, making a reverse C. "Wow," I said, and the beautiful Italian girl and I exchanged a look that said, How nice! How surprising! How puzzling!

The gator turned toward us and came our way along the surface of the bayou with smooth, deliberate thrusts of its tail. The water bulged off its head and body the way ocean water bulges off a surfacing submarine. "Eek!" cried the beautiful Italian girl, splashing me in her efforts to back-paddle.

"Look out!" I shouted, my razor-sharp reflexes coming into play. I understood within a fraction of a second that when a 500-pound gator rushes toward you and your friend, you should shout "Look out!" because that way your friend will know that such an animal is dangerous and definitely to be avoided.

Before the echo of my warning had faded, the alligator passed right between our boats, showering us with a mighty cascade of dark water as it dived down with one last flip of its tail. "Ohhhhhh!" cried the beautiful Italian girl, slapping frantically at the surface with her paddle.

"Come on!" I yelled, and we both started paddling madly back toward the car. She moaned and swore and cried all the way. I chivalrously stayed behind her, as if I could somehow defend her from the creature. I watched her thrash madly right up onto the concrete ramp, whereupon she and the boat fell over, and she wriggled out and scrambled back to the truck. I leapt out and followed her, looking at the water behind, where our wakes were already petering out and the water was settling back into a black mirror.

This is the hard part, the part that makes me think this story should be about something else, like the time Kate came home from a party and told me our friend Bruce had tried to kiss her. This is the part where the beautiful Italian girl gives me an angry, sodden look, then breaks into tears, and I open my arms and she puts her forehead on my shoulder and I murmur things like "I'm sorry" and "It's okay." And you're thinking that's not so bad, but then she raises her face to tell me something and without thinking—or maybe, in my confusion, thinking she's Kate—I kiss her mouth. Not for long, and not deeply, but certainly in a way that vaults us right past all of the decorum and courtesy that has so far dominated our acquaintance. Her lips felt thinner and harder than Kate's, which jolted me out of whatever trance made me think—not think, but sense that it was her, and so I broke off the kiss to give her a shy, alarmed look and a guilty "Sorry."

The beautiful Italian girl narrowed her eyes thoughtfully. "It's okay," she said, and smiled faintly before stepping away from me, head turned, to move around to the passenger door.

She sat in the truck while I walked wide-eyed back to the boats and the still water. What the hell? I thought. Such things never happened. Never.

I tried to think of an explanation. I had heard of hungry gators lunging for dogs in the fronts of canoes, had heard of children's legs in murky water briefly grasped and hand-fed Florida canal gators emboldened enough to snatch at divers, but even the biggest I had seen had always kept their distance, mostly fleeing in a panic the moment I appeared. I kept thinking as I dragged the kayaks back to the truck, gathered up gear, and let my heart slow its pace. Harry had once told me of a gator that had knocked his canoe over in a mad rush for the safety of deeper water...don't get between a gator and deep water...they'll take the most direct path, and if you're in the way...which was where the beautiful Italian girl and I had been...right. So while we had been racing back to the ramp with images of wide-open jaws and underwater death rolls, the poor monster had been lying still on the bottom, hoping we would not hurt it.

How do you get into the truck in which a beautiful Italian girl whom you have just kissed sits? What's the right posture, the right thing to say? When I don't know how to act, I tend to fall back on semi-conscious imitations. So I jumped into the truck, keys jangling, and used the voice of a jolly television father-figure to say, "Well, that was exciting, wasn't it?" I gave the task of driving back out to the dirt road more attention than it really deserved, but still I couldn't help glancing at the beautiful Italian girl and catching her half-rueful, half-bewildered expression.

This story could be about Kate. It should be. Lots of interesting things have happened to Kate. Once, for example, a guy at a party mistook her for a beautiful European girl and tried out his rusty German on her.

All the way home I struggled to think of something to talk about besides what had happened, but I wasn't willing to stoop so low as to make remarks about cloud formations or passing vehicles. There were more important things to say, like "Now that I think about it, that whole thing wasn't even real. It wasn't what it seemed," but the beautiful Italian girl and I did not talk at all. I pulled into the driveway and very deliberately set the parking brake. "Thank you for showing me that landscape," she said quietly, and got out of the car. The rest of the day she studied in her room, making no noise.

"See any gators?" Kate asked at dinner, seeming to address both the beautiful Italian girl and me. She and I exchanged a look that tripped my heart.

"Just one," I said, taking a big bite of broccoli. I chewed for a moment. "Remember that time you bought a twelve-dollar Coke in Paris?"

Kate just laughed. "Don't forget to get salsa next time you're at the store," she said.

Monday, the moment I came home from work, Kate handed Gina to me and hustled out to pick up the beautiful Italian girl from the university library. "We might stop for coffee," she called as the door closed.

Gina tugged at my necktie. "What do you want to do?" I asked. I let her pour the rice and the water into a pan, and while it cooked we lay on the floor of her room acting out fairy tales with stuffed animals. During dinner we talked about which animals fly, which ones swim, and which roam the earth. "How about some fruit?" I said, and there went another ten minutes. "Mom'll be home soon," I said, and we went back to her room again. The stuffed wolf cub wandered off away from the pig and the dragon's picnic and got lost in the woods, where it met a sarcastic kitten. The cub and the kitten had a long argument about where they might find some sort of enchanted house made of candy or vegetables and whether such houses were always (or only sometimes) occupied by evil witches. Up drove a recreational vehicle made entirely of potato chips and saltines. The pig was behind the wheel, and the dragon sat beside him. They all went home for ice cream, and Kate still had not come back. Gina and I had our own ice cream, and then I convinced her to get into a bath.

"You'd better not fall in love," Kate had joked on that first day, and I hadn't. Seventeen years I'd known Kate, and I could picture the look on her face as she sat over lattes with the beautiful Italian girl, getting the real story of the gator, the kiss.

A butterfly fluttered inside my ribcage when I heard the garage door go up. Kate and the beautiful Italian girl came breezing in, joking about American accents and Italian restaurants. The beautiful Italian girl got a drink of water, checked her watch, and excused herself to get ready for bed. "Sleep well," I called.

"What did you and Gina do?" Kate asked, pushing off her shoes and heading back to the bedroom.

"Not too much," I said, following her.

Kate shut the door, unbuttoned her blouse and draped it over the dresser, then sank down onto the bed, putting both hands over her face. "She's leaving," she sobbed, but quietly so that the beautiful Italian girl would not hear. "She says she found a place closer to the university and she's moving out tomorrow!"

"It's all right," I managed to say.

"But I don't understand why," she said. Her shoulders heaved with the crying. "I thought we were getting really close."

I sat down and put my arm around her. "Shh," I said, wondering how to say that I knew exactly how hard it is to love just one person for seventeen years, no matter who washes up on your doorstep.

"What did I do wrong?" Kate asked, and gave me a bleary look through her tears. "What did I do wrong?"

Qatar Is an Emirate

I never wash my car, but on the Sunday evening of Tessie's return I was out in front of the house with a bucket of soapy water and a worn out Jimi Hendrix T shirt, splashing soap across the corroded hood of my old Nissan. I probably missed a few spots, because my eyes kept shifting back to her end of the street. Twice I swore I saw her head of thick dark hair bobbing toward me, but it was someone else or an illusion created by the suburban dusk. Neighbor after neighbor passed by, enjoying the cool May air with dogs and kids in tow, and they all had to smile or say something— Dr. Borders from two doors down asked what I thought of the Saints' quarterback situation but moved on before I could tell him I thought football was a waste of energy. My face began to get tired from displaying a halfway polite smile. I was about to give up and head inside when I noticed a definite bustle down in front of Tess's house.

I ducked down to wash the tires. From such a distance she looked no different— the wavy hair, the body like a stick. She had to greet everyone, stopping in front of Mr. Richard's house, nodding and answering questions as he watered his azaleas. Mrs. Richard came out to hug Tess. When Tess finally waved and continued toward me, I scuttled around to the front of the car to wash the headlights. I could see her through my car's windows, and sure enough she was staring at my uncle's house as she approached. I took it as another good sign that she nearly ignored some kid on a bike who stopped and shyly welcomed her home.

I stood up when she was two doors down, but I stayed focused on the car, cleaning the antenna carefully. "Is that you?" I heard her say, the first time I'd heard her voice since she'd said good-bye back in December.

"Oh hey Tessie," I called, as if my heart hadn't migrated to my throat. "When did you get back?"

"To the States or to New Orleans?" she asked. "They had me at Fort Polk a few days."

"What was it like over there?" I leaned on the fender as casually as possible.

"Indescribable," she said eagerly. "The culture was neat. My friend Khalifa showed me all the sights. The sand was like powder though! It got in everything."

"Bet you're sick of sand," I said. "I'd offer you a beverage, but all we have is sand."

She laughed and stumbled down the steep lawn extension. "I wish you had been there, Phil. You would have loved the architecture, the food, everything. And I didn't have a camera."

"You'll have to tell me all about it," I said.

"Of course." She took a step back. "I'd better take off though. I was supposed to go see Melissa, and it's almost dark now."

I watched her walk away. She blended slowly into the grey light. I wanted to pour the bucket of water over my head for being so pushy. I'd blown it when I'd hinted that Tess should come inside, drape herself across the recliner in my room and talk for hours.

The day Tess had left, she'd shown up in the morning and said lightly, "Take a walk?" as if it weren't her last day, as if she shouldn't be doing other things, as if she weren't decked out in fatigues. It was December, gray rain threatening. We didn't say much until we'd crossed Orleans and left our isolated little neighborhood behind. We took our usual route, wandering under the big spooky oaks at the edge of City Park. "Think he'll back down?" she'd asked brightly, after a pause.

I knew I had to answer fast, as if there were only one possibility in my mind. "Got to," I pronounced.

"I probably won't be near the border anyway." She stood very still, studying the traffic, and for the twentieth time in a month I imagined stepping a little closer, pulling her into an embrace. All I could manage was to take one of her hands. That in itself was a milestone. Her delicate freckled hands. She surprised me by folding one arm around my neck and burying her face in my shoulder. It hurt. She pulled me off balance, and my neck cracked in protest. "You know that memorial, with the names..." she began, murmuring into my jacket.

"That was a whole different situation," I stated certainly.

"Really?" She sounded surprised, and looked into my face carefully as she unhooked her arm.

"Sure," I said, thinking fast. "The terrain, the politics...."

"I'm sure you're right," she said, but the crease between her eyebrows remained. I'd first noticed it a couple of weeks before. It was the width of a hair and just an inch tall, but I was sure it hadn't been there when I'd met her.

As we started back, she made an attempt at brave gaiety. "I hope I won't get bored," she said. "I might, sitting around in some kind of staging area. You'd better write me a lot of letters."

"Of course," I told her. "I'll be your Lakeview correspondent. Keep you up to date on all the latest lawn mowers, barbecued meats and what have you."

She was silent for a moment. She kicked a pine cone. "You'll still be here, won't you?" she asked. "I mean they won't kick you out for blowing this one semester."

"Right," I said, bluffing again. "I'll be back in the swing

of things soon."

"Good." She squeezed my hand, proving to me that this was actually happening, that our close friendship was making a slow transition to something else. As we neared her house I hoped for a quick resolution, imagining getting home and finding the TV full of the news that nothing would happen, the whole operation called off. Just in case though, I tried to think of some words or gesture that could bridge the upcoming interruption of months— a year? Suddenly we'd stopped before her house, facing one another. "Take care," she said gently, and I advised her to break a leg.

I made the mistake of not keeping my promise to her. A month after she left, I got a short letter with her new APO number. *Phil*, it began. *I miss you more than I've ever missed anything. I feel close to you though. I can't wait to see your smile....* It was embarrassing, so saccharine and conventional. It didn't sound like her, and it took things too far too quickly. She ended with, *I can't wait to see you!* and signed it *Love, Tess*. There were actual X's and O's at the bottom. Nothing about the war, the desert, the foreign land. She could just as easily have written from a Motel 6 in Arkansas.

I tried a variety of responses. *Dear Tess: I miss you too, one* ran. *I'd like to kiss you*. I tore that one up into pieces small enough to flush down the toilet. I tried being offhand and newsy, with no reference to her letter. I tried a strictly interrogative approach: *What's it like over there? How close to the border are you? How hot is it? See any three-hump camels?* Nothing I wrote fit the spirit of our clumsy embrace in City Park. I gave up trying, knowing I wouldn't even have to ask Tess to forgive me.

Her second letter came three and a half months later. It was very brief. *Phil: I get home on May 12. Tess.*

Monday, the day after her homecoming, I found Tess at

the lakefront. It took me a few hours to work up to it. I spent the morning in bed reading *A Walk in the Sun,* the latest in a series of books my uncle Bob had recommended since I'd drifted away from the University of New Orleans. I preferred mysteries, but suspected that as long as I kept educating myself with Bob's old paperbacks he'd tolerate my presence. Between chapters I parted the blinds and tried to tell if Tess' car was still out in front of her house. Bob crawled around below the window, pulling tiny weeds out of the flower bed.

At lunch Bob was absorbed in a new seed catalog. I weighed my options as I chewed. I considered passing by Tessie's with some excuse— Thought you might want to see some of the *Ellery Queens* that came while you were gone, or Have you tried starting your car since you got back? As if I knew how to revive cars.

I kept advising myself to wait until evening, to give her the chance to re-establish the routine we'd had all autumn. She had never made up reasons, but just knocked on the door and came in, or tapped at the window and asked if I was ready for a walk. She had come over most evenings, especially in November when it was clear she'd be off to defend Kuwait soon. I warned myself: Let her come to you, thinking maybe we'd rent *A Fish Called Wanda* or amble down Marshall Foch poking fun at all the senior Lakeview citizens in their Crown Vics.

Tess' mother answered the door. She told me she thought Tess had mentioned something about the lakefront. "How's school?" she asked fondly, before I could turn to go.

"Fine I guess," I replied, not bothering to explain.

I drove to the lake and found Tess on a park bench at the top of the seawall. When I first spotted her I kept driving, pretending not to see her. Half a mile later I turned the car around and promised myself I'd only stop if she was still there. The odds were heavily in my favor. There she was, with her feet drawn up and her bony legs folded under her. I parked at the curb behind her.

"I thought that was you," I called. She twisted around, squinting as she watched me pick my way through the half-hardened mud surrounding the bench.

"I'm looking at the water," she confided as I sat down opposite her. "I haven't seen much lately."

"I'll bet." Right away I thought she wasn't being herself, like she was forcing words out of her mouth or trying to guide the conversation.

"My friend Khalifa didn't understand what a lake was," she laughed. "He's from Qatar, which occupies a peninsula that juts from Eastern Arabia into the Persian Gulf. So he's seen water of course, but I just couldn't explain the concept of lake."

"He's from Guitar?"

"Qatar. It's an emirate. It has little natural water." She stretched her mile-long legs out in front of her. "A lake. 'How exotic,' he'd say. That was his phrase."

Maybe if I hadn't played along— if I'd stopped her right there by saying Why are you talking like this? and Look, I'm really sorry I didn't write— things would have been easier. We could have gotten down to the business of developing the romance we'd begun in the fall. But I just played along, hoping she'd cut it out. "I guess it is exotic," I remarked.

"Not to me," she laughed. "Isn't that funny? To me it's boring. I've seen it a thousand times. To Khalifa it'd be a wonder. He'd get all excited and forget his English like he does."

Without really deciding to, I tried for a Hail Mary play. "I came here to say good-bye," I said, surprised at my own words.

"Oh?" She blinked at me. "Why? What do you mean?"

"I'm going back to Lafayette, and I don't know if I can come back in the fall." I spoke to the lake. I wasn't exactly lying, but I was certainly improvising.

"You transferring to USL?" she asked.

"Not exactly. I never really went back to school."

Tess exhaled and stared at her shoes. I slid over the rough wood and sat next to her. "I blew it," I murmured, as glumly as possible. "Now I don't know what to do with my life. I don't want to work offshore again. I'm sick of being a loser."

"You'll be all right." She toed a shell out of the mud.

I saw my chance. "I hope you're right," I breathed, and leaned against her, swinging one arm out to capture her in the crook of my elbow. She froze. I tried not to admit it, but I could feel her distance herself. She was as stiff as your average tree.

"I promised to help my mom," she said, after I'd released her. She stood. "With the garden and all."

"Sure," I said, and she strode off abruptly, leaving me to study the ridged mud and pick flakes of thick green paint off the bench.

"Does Mr. Clifton have a spark plug wrench I could borrow?" I asked Tessie's mother early that evening.

"Oh, I wouldn't know," she laughed. "And I'm not sure Jerry's here. Let me call Tess." As she spoke, Tess wandered into the foyer behind her, carrying a peeled carrot.

"I'll help you look." She squeezed past her mother and led me around the house. I followed, half of me congratulating myself on a successful ploy, the other half telling myself to be ashamed.

We stopped in the doorway of her father's garage workshop. The light was green and cool. "What kind of wrench?"

"Spark plug."

"What you need it for?"

I hesitated. I hadn't thought this through very well. "One of my sparks needs unplugging."

Tess pointed out some likely drawers, and I dutifully shuffled to the tool chest. I wasn't sure what a spark plug wrench looked like. Mr. Clifton seemed to own dozens of unusual wrenches.

"You ever see the spark plug on an M1?" Tessie asked suddenly, in that unnatural voice. "That's a tank, an M1 tank."

"Nah." I took a close look at a torque wrench.

"Khalifa worked on tanks. He's a mechanic. Not the M1, their tanks were, I don't know, British I think. Yeah, because in 1916 Qatar became a British protectorate."

"Figures." I found a wrench with an especially deep socket. It looked possible. I closed the drawers.

Tessie pressed on. "And listen to this: they first discovered oil in 1939, in Western Qatar. Before that, Qataris made a living by raising camels, fishing or pearl diving." She was silhouetted in the doorway, gesturing with the remains of her carrot. "And now Qatar ranks among the richest nations in terms of average income per person."

I gave her a long stare before I said, "So?"

"It reminds me of you, that's all," she said, still looking up and out into the branches of an oak tree. "Some day you'll find your niche and all."

"I did find the wrench," I said. "That's a start."

"You seemed so down earlier today, and I know the feeling. I mean, I've got to get out of my parents' house again, out of New Orleans. But just think of Qatar— you might have to tend a few camels before the oil pops up."

"That's what my grandfather always said. Those very words. Should we take a walk?" That was the punch line of my ploy.

"Oh no," she said, finally meeting my eyes. "I got a letter from Qatar today and I want to answer it tonight. You should see Khalifa's handwriting."

"All right." I backed away, retreating into the yard. "Hasta la bagel."

I walked the two-minute walk up our street as quickly as possible. Still it was torment. My face felt hot, and I knew everyone could tell what had just happened and how miserable I was. Mr. Richard seemed to stare at me with unnatural curiosity as he stood trimming his bushes. A kid from the next street over swerved his bike at me and made me jump. I was at a low point.

Bob looked up from filling his watering can as I came up the walk. "What's that?" he asked.

"What do you mean?" My voice was loud and strained. I fought it down to say, "Oh, this. It's either a spark plug wrench or a wrench plug spark, I forget which."

Bob laughed, freeing me to rush to my room and bury myself in the lead story of the latest *Alfred Hitchcock*.

In the morning, during the prelude to a thunderstorm, everything became clearer. I stood on the front stoop and watched leafy debris rattle down the street, swept by sudden gusts. The sky turned greenish grey and distant rumbles came quickly closer, slamming the air with sounds of destruction. Of course, I thought. Of course.

The sun was back out by early afternoon, making the pavement steam and simulating late July. I could lie here all day, I thought, stretched across the couch with a new novel. There was nothing to pull me away from the soft cushions and cooled air.

Later I decided to test my new resolve. I can do this, I told myself. No more borrowing things, making up excuses. No more awkward overtures. I laced my All-Stars tight and left the house.

I hesitated when I reached the sidewalk. The natural thing to do, the nonchalant thing, would be to turn left and head up the street toward Navarre, passing Tessie's house on the way to Weaver's. Still, I thought. Why take a chance so soon? I decided to wait and test myself on the way back. So instead I went right and made a slight detour around the block to avoid the white house with the dark green trim.

The girl behind the counter at Weaver's had wonderful lips and naturally arched eyebrows. She was the first person I could pick out as I felt my way through the dim interior. As the bright-sidewalk blindness cleared, her face emerged. "You okay?" she asked.

"I'm snow-blind," I said. "I've been out on the tundra."

"Awful hot tundra."

"That's why I need a huge Coke."

"All we have is large." She smiled. So did I. When she turned away, I realized how tall and solid she was— none of this anorexic girlishness. No sharp-cornered bones.

I sat by the window watching the lazy traffic on Navarre. After she'd taken care of the guy who'd come in behind me, she ducked under the counter and moved easily around the room with a rag, wiping tables. She caught me watching and waved to me. Yeah, I thought. All right. Yeah.

The way she'd brightened when I'd said good-bye stayed in my mind as I walked home. I walked quickly, taking the direct route. It was very simple until I came to the T where our street began. The Cliftons were just a few doors from the corner. It would have been conspicuous to cross the street when Bob's house was on the same side. The thought of Tess at a window or sitting on the swing or trotting out of the house calling me caused my step to falter. I knelt to un-tie and re-tie one of my shoes before I turned the corner, frantically wondering what to say.

I tried to keep my eyes on my feet, but found that as I came close I could still see her house and her car at the edge of my vision. For a moment I turned my head to study the Voights' house across the way, but there was still the problem of her white Tercel at the curb. Finally I closed my eyes. The sidewalk was level and straight, so it was easy. In the red darkness behind my lids Tessie's sharp face began to form, but then I was past and could open my eyes. The street reappeared and all was well. But when I tried to picture the Weaver's girl and revive the feeling I'd had, nothing happened.

The call came just after the sun had gone behind the trees. I had a sense of doom as I took the phone from Bob's hand. "Phil? Jerry Clifton," a voice said. "Tess mentioned something about one of my wrenches."

"Right."

"Listen, are you finished with it? I have a policy about my tools."

I told him I'd wrenched all the plugs I could wrench and agreed to bring it right over. What could I do? The man had a policy. I promised myself that if Tessie popped up, my policy would be to turn my head, close my eyes, or do whatever it took.

She didn't pop up until after I'd greeted Mr. Clifton, thanked him, handed him the wrench and turned to go. In fact I had reached the street by the time she came out from the back yard calling, "Phil! Philadelphia Phil!"

I was far enough away to pretend not to hear. I even broke into a slow trot, figuring that if she asked I'd claim to want to catch something on TV. When she caught me, I slowed to a walk but kept my eyes forward.

"I just— I'm excited and I wanted to tell you," she gasped.

"I'm trying to catch a movie on HBO," I told her.

She ignored me, keeping her eyes on the sky. "It's so— remember Khalifa, my Qatari friend? Now that the war's over, he's going to be an airline pilot, so he'll be able to visit me. You'll get to meet him. I hope I won't be too embarrassed showing him around Lakeview— all these boring houses, boring people."

I wondered if I was being insulted. I ignored that thought and instead pounced on an inconsistency. "How'd he get to be an airline pilot so fast?"

"Well, he was a fighter pilot, and now—"

I stopped walking. I really thought I had her cornered, and I braced myself for all the truth to come pouring out. "A fighter pilot?"

"Yeah. Harriers. British Harriers." Her face was vivid and older, and I wondered if she was wearing makeup.

"Before you said he was a tank mechanic."

"Oh." She laughed, crossed her ankles, glanced back toward her house. "You know, he's so good with machines, being a pilot. He used to hang out by the tank garages all the time...." She smiled hopefully.

"I thought you were back at some supply thing," I said, thinking *Anytime, Tess. Just say the word.*

But she kept it up. "Oh, I was. We had an airstrip. Transports had to land, you know."

"So is a Harrier a transport?"

"It's a fighter," she said, irritated. "In 1916, Qatar became a British protectorate." She stared at her hands, touching her fingers as if she were counting. "Qatar became an independent nation in 1971. Don't you get it?" she snorted, gesturing toward my end of the street. "I mean after all that time, don't you think they'd still have ties to the British?"

"Come off it, Tess. Stop lying," is what I should have said. But who has the guts to say that kind of thing? Instead I said, "My movie just started," and stalked off.

"He lives in Doha," Tess called after me. "Doha is the capital and largest city of Qatar. Much of Doha has a modern appearance."

I drove up to the lakefront to fume. I ignored Bob, who

was spreading pine bark under the crape myrtle. My car sneezed twice, then ran evenly and loudly. I popped the clutch without much result and lurched away. Storming up Canal in third, I swerved viciously around potholes and slowpokes. At the lakefront I found the day slowly dying. There were still a few strolling couples, and the last low-rider trucks were rolling out, woofers pumping. One sailboat jerked toward the marina under power, its mainsail hanging useless.

I sat on top of the seawall watching small waves suck at the bottom step. This is not how I planned it, I realized, thinking beyond Tess. How did I plan it? Did I plan it? I couldn't remember. I remembered how great it felt to be nineteen and living alone, being flown out to drilling platforms. I always had too much money then, though I was never sure exactly how much. I thought I was just where I wanted to be for life. That kind of feeling is hard to kill, but it did slowly fade and go sour. I had to do a lot of planning, wrangling and hoping to get the feeling back. It returned the day I moved into Bob's house: I had a big wad of savings, I was registered at the university, and a willowy black-haired girl was talking to me as I unloaded the car. Now what? The money was still there, but school was a total loss. So was Tess, either way— with a flesh and blood Qatari suitor or with an invented one. I reached behind me and scooped up a handful of stray paving shells. As I threw them out into the water, gulls gathered overhead, shouting in confusion.

I started to drive back slowly, resigned. At a stoplight I watched an old couple in a Lincoln ahead of me, the way their heads swiveled in alarm as if they were lost. They've lived here forty years, I realized, and they don't know where they are. What's keeping me here? I decided to pack the car immediately and leave by dawn.

In the midst of wondering whether there were any apartments open at my old complex and trying to remember where the phone numbers of some of my old co-workers might be, I discovered that I'd driven the usual route back to Bob's house, the route that would take me to Tessie's end of the street. I'll just do what I did before, I decided as I approached the T intersection. I held my eyes open long enough to get straightened out after the left turn. Just go slow and keep it on line, I told myself, closing my eyes. It'll be over in a few seconds.

I hit the brake at the first jolt. Metal screeched. A big hand shoved me forward. The steering wheel jerked to the left. The motor died. When I opened my eyes, I saw Tessie's white Tercel in the dusk beside me, tilted against my Nissan's front fender, close enough to touch. "Damn it!" I shouted. "What were you doing?" But her car was empty. "Tess?" I called, mystified until I saw where I was. The Clifton's sycamore was towering above me, the Tercel, the Nissan.

Mrs. Clifton startled me when she leaned in the passenger window. "Phil? Are you all right? Goodness, how did it happen?"

"I was going pretty slow," I said apologetically, climbing toward her over the seat.

"Did you hit your head?" she asked, setting her hand on my arm as I stood up.

"I don't think so. Tessie's car...she's going to hate me now."

"Nonsense, Phil," she cooed, leading me toward the house. "Tess really likes you. She's the forgiving kind, as they say. Come on." She took me inside, sat me down in the kitchen, fed me ice water and insisted that I recite my social security number, birth date, and a reverse alphabet. I kept waiting for Mr. Clifton or Tess to appear in the hallway and ask what was going on. "I should go tell my uncle," I said, once she was satisfied my head hadn't been dented.

"Why don't you write a note to Tess first?" She studied

my face with gentle eyes.

"She's not here?" I asked, relieved.

"She and her dad went to Harry's Ace Hardware. Here." She snatched a pen from a canister by the phone, then stood, taking my elbow and guiding me carefully. "There's a notepad on her desk," she said, parking me in front of Tessie's bedroom door. She opened it and gave me a shove.

I felt overwhelmed. I'd never seen her room before, even though she'd lounged on the floor of my room or in the recliner for hours, helping me with a computer program, watching videos or just laughing and talking. I'd never thought to imagine her room. It was oddly girlish: a white lace-trimmed bed, carefully arranged books, a teddy bear, porcelain figurines, neo-impressionist prints on the walls. I sat gingerly at the tidy Formica desk and took a notepad from its place in the little Plexiglas organizer.

Tess—

Don't get too mad. I crunched your car. I'll fix it for you. I built quite a few model cars back in junior high, so it should be a cinch.

—Phil.

I looked for an obvious place to leave it. The desk was too far from the door. I tried the pillow, but somehow the note looked too intimate tucked under a corner of the lace pillowcase. Instead I put it on a book lying on her bedside table. As I stepped away I recognized it as one of the volumes of a compact encyclopedia. I was almost out the door before I thought to check the spine. Q-R.

That probably doesn't mean anything, I told myself, knowing it probably did. I scribbled a postscript.

P.S. I leave tomorrow on the 6 a.m. Greyhound. Won't see you. Bye forever.

I found Mrs. Clifton in the living room, splitting the blinds at the front window. I moved up next to her and peered out too. Tessie and her father were circling the two wounded vehicles, looking dazed. "You'd better go out there," she murmured.

It was the hardest thing I could remember doing— opening the door and walking down the front walk, waiting for them to notice me. Tess saw me first and called out gladly, "Phil!" Her father gave me a stern look and strode past, slamming the door on his way in.

I slumped against the trunk of the sycamore, hanging my head. Tess put her hands on her knees, placing her face in my line of sight. "Sorry," I muttered.

"I can't believe you did this," she giggled. "You really like me, don't you?"

"Yeah." I shrugged, puzzled.

"Oh cheer up," she said, shoving me gently. "I mean look at our cars! Like Siamese twins, joined at the hood."

I smiled half-heartedly. Tess grabbed my hand and pulled. "Come on," she said. "Let's take a walk."

We didn't say much at first, except Tess said, "What is it with these sprinklers?" grinning at me as we passed the fifth lawn that was still being watered in the near darkness. I kept waiting for her to either release some new information on another charming aspect of Khalifa's personality or finally realize that I'd seriously damaged her car and turn on me. I had too much on my mind to register where we were going and didn't notice that she'd led me to the oak-laden rim of City Park until we were there, dodging Spanish moss and tripping over roots.

"This is the most intriguing thing that's happened to me in years," she said suddenly.

"Huh?"

"The cars. Your sculpture. 'Convergence,' by Phil Broussard."

"Saudi wasn't intriguing?"

"Oh sure, at first," she said. "But I mean, I didn't see

much of it. I got so bored after about two weeks. A bunch of sand, a bunch of equipment, a few normal-looking buildings a mile away— I've learned more about Islamic architecture from the *World Book*."

I could barely see her in the deep twilight shadow of the oaks. I tried to make out her expression as I said carefully, "But you met...some interesting people, right? You made friends over there."

"I wish!" Tessie gushed. "Oh God, I wish I could say I met anyone interesting." She stomped forward, laughing. "I mean the villagers were pretty westernized. This little Qatari infantry force drove through one day, but...that was nothing really."

I could have taken that as a confession and let her off the hook right there. But I wanted to make sure. "So when's Khalifa coming to see you?" I asked gently.

Tess exhaled through her nose. We stopped walking, and she leaned back against the trunk of an old oak, facing me. Her eyes were just shadows but I knew she meant it when she said, "Phil, I'm sorry about Khalifa, about that whole Khalifa thing."

"All right," I whispered, moving closer. We put our arms around each other's necks and stood that way for a moment, trying to erase the past six months.

We walked back to our street in tranquil silence. Before I left Tess at her doorstep, we both turned to study my automotive masterpiece. The streetlight overhead bathed it in a circle of light. "First in a series," I murmured.

Two minutes later, I was exactly half the distance between Tessie's and my uncle's houses. Someone came trotting up behind me. I stopped in the middle of the street. It was Tess, barefoot, breathing hard. "Phil," she panted, stopping. "I found this in my room." She handed me the note I'd written.

"Um." I tried to think.

"Let me catch me breath." She smiled, patting her chest. "Hoo." She swiped at her eyes. "I couldn't read the P.S.," she said at last, keeping her mouth in the shape of a smile.

"Oh yeah," I said. "Let me see. It's sort of dark out here." I held the paper close to my face.

"Something about a bus?"

"Right. No, I think it says, 'Now that you've wrecked my car, I guess I'm stuck in Lakeview for a while.'"

"Oh." She sounded relieved. "That's what I thought."

"Here." I handed the note to her, watching carefully. She kept her eyes on mine and casually wadded it up tight in one hand.

Out There in TV Land

It just so happened that Brandt stopped working on his dissertation, *Godzilla as Atomic Metaphor,* and left his falafel-scented apartment to head toward his Aunt Eileen's beige-brick suburban stronghold at about the same time Wallace clicked off Paul Harvey and emerged from his so-called workshop to make a motorized voyage to his Cousin Eileen's house. Brandt cranked his old Hunta Civet, with its pigeon-decorated hood and the greenish sheen, with a secret pride. The fuzziness, the odd clickings and rattles, gave the car character and conferred a certain amount upon him. Lighting a Llama, he kept his eyes cast down to disguise the smug feeling from any passersby— not that he saw any. A few miles to the north, Wallace drove alertly, smiling faintly, especially when his eyes fell on that new LCD compass on the dashboard, the one he'd ordered from an ad in the back of *Leader's Ingest.* As much as possible, he kept his conversion van on a southeast course, even changing lanes rather abruptly on Perkins to make that baby flash SE again.

Aunt/Cousin Eileen had done everything she could to keep Wallace and Brandt from coming to her house at the same time, to stop the boulder she'd set rolling a few days earlier from careening out of control. When old Eric had died, mere weeks after investing in a brand new Itsasushi television, she hadn't been sure what to do with it. It now sat precariously in a soft chair in her living room, wider than any person who'd ever used that chair, dwarfing it, its black plastic bulk somehow ominous despite the floral upholstery, curtains, and carpeting. She'd merely been thinking out loud when Brandt had called about something the day of the funeral, wondering what she would do with it, then finding herself asking if he wanted it. To her, "I'll think about it" didn't mean he would be on his way to pick it up less than a week later, and there'd been no harm in mentioning it to Wallace, who said he wanted it before she could get around to asking him. The memory of this morning's phone calls still echoed in her ear: she could hear the gruff, obstinate way Wallace had said, "If he gets there first he can have it," and the mysterious silence on Brandt's end when she'd told him she might have accidentally promised the TV to his uncle. Secretly she was rooting for Brandt, because he was young and because Wallace was a pack rat who had ten garage-sale televisions in various states of repair and disrepair.

She had even told Wallace to come around four, an hour after Brandt was to come, forgetting Wallace's tendency to be early and Brandt's fashionable tardiness. Thus it was that the Civet and the conversion van met in Eileen's driveway, and both men stepped out at the same time. Both smiled, exaggerating the need to squint in the bright sunlight. Brandt eyed Wallace's pale blue ElastaBelt shorts, yellowish skinny legs, beige socks pulled way up high, yellow golf shirt. And then there was the van, Wallace's crowning glory. For years Brandt had been dying to know if there was shag carpeting on the ceiling in the back, but the windows were too dark, and he was not about to ask. Wallace took note of Brandt's frayed baggy jeans, huge shirt, poorly trimmed beard, and the whatchacallits on his feet—Mexican sandals . . .Hibachis? And then there was the eyebrow ring. A guy like that probably had a tattoo on his heiney.

"You here about the TV?" Wallace asked.

Brandt stuck his hand out with false gusto. "Top o' the morning to ye, Uncle Wallace!"

Wallace hesitated, then shook Brandt's hand, wondering how clean the hand of a man with a car that dirty could be, and what drug would make a man think P.M. was A.M. "Guess we'd better let Eileen settle this," he said.

Their presence in her living room taxed Eileen's hostessing skills. She did what she could, bringing them iced tea and filling the tense air with cheerful small talk about the warm front and Eric's funeral and the number of acorns in the yard. Finally she had to stop clattering around in the kitchen and sit down between them on the couch. There was a moment of silence in which all three of them avoided glancing toward the TV. Eileen took a deep breath and said, "Well, there it is." Wallace and Brandt merely nodded, there being no arguing with her statement.

"Let's cut it in half," Brandt suggested.

"Do you watch a lot of television?" Eileen asked.

"A VCR is absolutely essential in my field of study," Brandt said seriously. "It's impossible to survive without one. Mine is hooked up to an old black and white, which is sufficient for some of the early Kaiju films, most notably the original *Godzilla* featuring a young Raymond Burr."

Wallace interrupted. "They got this new super slow motion where you can see the stitches on the ball and drops of sweat fly when the guy gets hit with a right hook. Only problem is none of my TVs is clear enough. Even with cable my best one is all green on one side." He turned to Brandt. "Sounds to me like you don't watch TV, though. Just movies."

"If I had an antenna I'd watch quite a bit, especially next semester, when I'm taking a seminar on the advertising image. I get my news from the *Morning Advocate,* but for certain news the lag time is a little inconvenient."

"I like Dan Preference on channel fourteen," Wallace volunteered.

Eileen gave her tea a vigorous stir, and given the awkward

tension it was enough to distract both men. They turned toward her slightly, and she felt obliged to speak. "I won't watch the news anymore. It's just as violent as everything else."

Wallace snorted. "They'll never learn to stop shooting each other."

"You mean the Serbs and Croats?" Brandt was stiff, eyes afire.

"Them too."

Brandt leaned forward to see around Eileen. "The white separatists and the FBI?"

Eileen did what she could to defuse the situation, brightly asking if anyone needed more tea. Would they enjoy some of those lemon cookies she'd bought at Piggly Wiggly? There was no answer, and her suggestion obliged her to go into the kitchen. Hoping to keep them from saying anything to each other while she was gone, she shouted that perhaps they should make sure the TV worked before they decided anything. But when she returned with the cookies, Wallace had started one of his tirades, and Brandt was slouched down, eyes closed, jaw clenched, looking surprisingly homeless.

"Most of it's junk," Wallace was saying. "Except for CNN and sports, all they have is a bunch of dirty sitcoms cooked up by those sex maniacs out in Hollywood. Then there's those cop shows with naked bodies all over the place. Who wants to see a naked cop? If I want a laugh I might watch Garson, but of course he's gone now. But that Jalen O. is a pretty nice young feller."

Brandt stirred, opening his eyes and sitting up straighter. "What about *Unsolved Rescues,* and *America's Funniest Police Videos?*" he sneered.

"Oh yeah. That's reality. Anything that's reality I like—sports, the news, talk shows."

"It is an interesting trend—reality television," Brandt conceded. "As if Western civilization had begun to exhaust its capacity for narrative invention."

"Yeah. You like *911 Live*?"

"I don't like any of it."

"Then why you want a TV?"

The breath Brandt took was the kind Dizzy Gillespie would take before blowing. "I wanna get me one of them there television sets so's I can watch me some sex-maniac sitcoms on that there channel tin!"

"You notice how there's a lot of nigger sitcoms nowadays?" Wallace asked, smiling first at Brandt, then at Eileen.

Brandt's eyes widened and he leaned away from Wallace. He groaned, and the groan became an incoherent shout as he stood up. "I knew it! You always find a way to do this." He gestured from the television to Wallace and back. "You deserve each other. That's all I have to say. You deserve each other."

If he had waited for Wallace's and Eileen's reactions, Brandt would have seen Wallace smiling obliviously and shrugging at Eileen, who was developing a rather crestfallen expression. But he didn't wait, and before Eileen could stand up the front door had slammed, and before she could open it the Hunta Civet was revving weakly as it drifted down the driveway.

Eileen wished Wallace would leave too, and somewhere the hospitality fairy must have waved her wand because after a few silent moments he stood up, draining the sweet paste out of the bottom of his tea glass. He smacked his lips, sighing, and she felt like smacking them herself. "Whelp," he chirped. "I can't load that thing by myself, and I'm not sure I want it if he's going to get all high and mighty about it. Can't miss the five o'clock news anyway." She was so relieved to be leading him to the door that she could only murmur a perfunctory "Come back any time" as he made his way out. He clambered boyishly up into the conversion van and drove away slowly, watching the compass flash NW.

I'll just give the TV to charity, Eileen thought, with uncharacteristic spitefulness. The thought stayed with her for nearly a week, in which time the bulky black appliance sulked in its chair, fancy and unwanted. She wasn't about to call either of them about picking it up, not after the way they'd acted, but neither was she about to call her sister or give in to the greedy hints the neighbor dropped whenever she saw the TV. Wallace called on a Tuesday, ostensibly to inform her that if she wanted he would order two Global Multi-Band Radios from an ad he'd seen in the Sunday *Charade*, thereby saving himself $29.95 and offering her access to Voice of the USA, Radio Free Eurasia, and Russian weather forecasts. When she declined politely, he said something about letting her go, then casually asked whether Brandt had come over with any of his scummy friends to pick up the Itsasushi. "You think he still wants it?" he asked, and Eileen caved in to her conciliatory instincts.

"I don't know if he wants it," she sighed. "And he probably doesn't know if you want it. Look, why don't you go over there one day and try to settle it with him? You might have to apologize, but isn't that better than having this argument between family?"

Wallace hissed into the phone before he spoke. "Apologize for what? I'll go over there if he invites me."

And so again she was playing the role of peacemaking go-between, calling Brandt and making it sound like Wallace was willing to come over and discuss things, then calling Wallace and claiming that Brandt had sounded like he wouldn't mind, then calling Brandt to find out if Friday afternoon was a good time and saying she thought Wallace was sorry about what he'd said. She supposed all this made her a liar a few times over and hoped God allowed lying for the sake of family harmony.

Wallace showed up at Brandt's door a good thirty minutes early, wearing a look of aggressive disgust. "There was a roach out here," he complained, gesturing down the dusty hallway.

"There are more in here," Brandt replied, taking note of Wallace's plaid pants. He hurried back to the loveseat, remote in hand.

Wallace hovered, glancing at a dinette chair in the corner but not taking a seat. He poked at the curtains distastefully, eyeing the street below. "This used to be a nice area," he said. "You know that? A lot of nice homes, nice yards and gardens, quiet people. You could take a walk at night without worrying about some—"

"Please," Brandt said, intent on the screen. He clicked a button and the television came to life, emitting a hoarse roaring hoot.

Wallace furrowed his brow. "Wait a second. That's that monster." He sidled around and stood next to the loveseat.

"Godzilla. Now here comes Mothra."

"They don't show those anymore. I wish they would, instead of all those bikini movies and Jap karate movies. Monster movies are wholesome, because they're not real."

"That makes sense," Brandt said, rolling his eyes. "Actually, they're allegories for Japan's struggle to come to grips with the nuclear age. Raymond Burr's voice-over at the beginning of the first Godzilla movie could just as easily be about the bomb that leveled Hiroshima as Godzilla. Ironically, Godzilla defends the Earth in a few of the later movies—the equivalent of the destructive power of the atom being turned to peaceful uses in power plants and laboratories."

Now it was Wallace's turn to roll his eyes. "Whatever," he said, and they both watched Mothra blow Godzilla around like so much lint with a few flaps of her clumsy wings. "So this is why you need a big fancy television."

"Color is a key aspect of any system of symbols. And unfortunately, I can't remember whether Godzilla's ray is blue or green."

Wallace brightened. "Look, I've got a nice color jobbie I picked up at a garage sale. Why don't I give it to you, and I'll take the Itsasushi."

"I don't want a fucked-up old TV where everyone's face is orange," Brandt snorted. "I need accurate color."

Tiny particles of spit flew from Wallace's mouth. He seemed to be having trouble exhaling through his clenched-up lips and reddening face. "Ppppp!" he stated, and then his voice came out high and angry. "You've got some nerve, sonny boy! You think I came over here to be insulted and cursed out with the most vile language I've ever heard, when I came over here to try to be nice and work things out with you, all for Eileen's sake, and you come out with this trash? I ought to wash your mouth out, but you probably don't even have any soap!"

Brandt blinked. "What's wrong?"

"Oh, very funny! You always think you're so smart and hilarious, don't you?" He stomped to the door, half-accidentally kicking over a low pile of books by the stereo, yanked the door open, left it open, and radiated umbrage all the way to his van and all the way home.

Eileen called Brandt the next day, hoping for an update on the peace accord. "I don't know. He freaked out about something," he told her. She was just as mystified by what Wallace said. "Our nephew is well on his way to spending an eternity in Hell," he fumed. When she asked what he'd done, he'd only say, "I can't repeat it, especially to a lady as outstanding as yourself."

Annoyed, she left them alone for nearly a week. But then she sensed that the length of time between her flower-arranging classmate having her over for lunch and her own reciprocating invitation was reaching a point of awkwardness that would soon become irreparable. On the other hand, she would be deeply embarrassed to let Mildred see her living room in such a state, with her best chair obliterated by the Itsasushi. She supposed the TV was the rock and Wallace and Brandt collectively comprised a hard place, unless one them was the rock and the other the hard place. Or was Mildred the hard place? She sat down with a glass of iced tea to try to stop thinking about it, and picked up the phone.

It had been easiest to lure them back to her house with the promise of food. She told Brandt to come around eleven and Wallace to come around noon, for dinner Saturday. The preparations were complex. She plugged in the TV and found that it didn't receive very well with no antenna. She found some rabbit ears at Gall-Mart, then found that the remote was non-functional—it was still in its little baggie, batteryless. Fortunately, batteries were available at Piggly Wiggly, where she also bought corn, a pork roast, sweet potatoes, dinner rolls, lettuce and tomatoes, pecans, milk, Coke, butter beans, and other essentials. She did most of the cooking the night before, then decided at about six A.M. to smoke a chicken as well.

Just as she'd hoped, Wallace and Brandt arrived within minutes of one another. She was still asking Brandt about school and getting him to retrieve the gravy boat from a high cabinet when Wallace came in, whistling a greeting. The transition from kitchen chit-chat to living-room sit-down went smoothly, Eileen explaining that she just needed a minute to make the gravy and they could relax for a few minutes. She'd laid out the remote just so on the coffee table, and as she'd hoped, Brandt picked it up as he sat down.

"Jesus wasn't afraid to say, 'I can dig it,'" a man was saying, but Brandt quickly jumped it to the next station. Animated kitchen appliances wearing macho armor were conferring in some sort of spaceship or castle.

"Wait, who was that?" Wallace asked, leaning forward in his chair. "Go back."

"Okay," Brandt said, flicking to a basketball game.

"Oops," he deadpanned. His thumb punched the button again, and a woman appeared. The caption under her image identified her as Tina: Swallowed Sheet Metal to Regain Abusive Husband. "Wow," Brandt sighed, upping the volume.

"Of course it hurt," Tina was saying, swiping at sweaty tears. "It hurt very much. But I love him. I love him very much."

"Which one is this?" Wallace asked.

"I think it's Nikki Rake."

Sure enough, Nikki's familiar image flashed onto the screen. "Okay Tina, there's a question for you. Go ahead." Standing in the audience, she thrust a club-like mic in a woman's face.

"First of all, I'd like to say I know what you're going through because my father was an alcoholic which is not the same thing but it caused us a lot of pain and my brother and I would do weird things like burn the macaroni on purpose just to get his attention, and second of all, how did you swallow it? I mean, did you snip it up into little pieces first, or was it like one big thing?"

"Have mercy," Wallace murmured.

"You ever seen this show before?" Brandt asked.

Wallace nodded slowly. "Many times, many times."

"It's got to be the most outrageous."

"It certainly is. Look at her." Now it was Janet: Glued Self to Ex-Boyfriend's Car.

"I used epoxy," Janet was saying. "My clothes stuck really well but not my skin. But I was inside. It's not like I was on the hood or anything." She laughed.

Eileen stalked quietly into the living room and stood behind Brandt and Wallace, happy to see them getting along so well, both of them leaning forward intently, not talking, seeming to commune through Nikki's show.

"I wish I had a pen and a paper," Wallace said feverishly, as the camera turned to Rosa: Painted Self Hunter Green to Please Alcoholic Mother.

"Here." Eileen backed into the foyer and took the pad and pencil from the phone stand. Wallace took them and began writing furiously, head bobbing as he looked from the screen to the paper and back again. "What's it for?" she asked.

"Names. I need their names so I can include them in my prayers."

"Jesus Christ," Brandt said.

Eileen saw the warning glance Wallace shot at Brandt, who didn't notice, and she saw Wallace point the pencil impatiently, pursing his lips. He let his hand fall, shaking his head resignedly. "Dinner's ready," she said.

"Hold on," Brandt said, at the same time Wallace said, "Wait a minute." She sighed and sat between them, waiting to hear from happy, smiling Lynette: Gave Blow Job to Get Out of Speeding Ticket.

"I don't think we want to see this," Eileen gasped, as the screen went black.

Brandt let the remote clatter onto the coffee table. "No, we don't."

Wallace sat wide-eyed, pencil poised over his prayer list. "Ugh," he said at last.

All three of them seemed to forget what they were doing for a moment. Brandt rubbed the back of his neck, while Wallace folded the list and solemnly handed the pencil to Eileen. No one looked at the dead television or anything near it. Eileen was the first to snap out of it. "Food's ready," she reminded them, and Wallace shot up out of his seat eagerly. Brandt sauntered off to the bathroom, Wallace took his place at the table, and Eileen tended to a few last details. They were apart for a few minutes, each alone with their thoughts. "I'm not sure I have room for such a big TV anyway," Brandt offered, seating himself.

"Oh, I'll help you put it in there, move the furniture around if we have to," Wallace countered.

"I was thinking you should take it."

"Listen, I've got a bunch of TV's already. What do I need another one for?"

"I really don't want it."

"Me neither."

"Well, you're certainly not leaving it with me!" Eileen cried angrily. "I want one of you to take it out of here, today. Take it down to Goodwill or the Redemption Navy."

"Put an ad in the paper," Wallace suggested.

"A donation would be tax deductible," Brandt pointed out.

Eileen rapped her fork against the table impatiently. "We can sort this out later. Now would someone please hurry up and ask the blessing?"

Don't Put Me Down

Nia had bought most of the loose stamps that littered the top drawer of Edwin's desk, and peering down at the brittle curls of paper, he admired her taste. There was a good variety: some flowers, some birds, a few cartoon characters and a handful from the American Talk Show Hosts series: Winfrey, Povich and others, most shown in profile, mouth open, mic raised to lips. She was like that about everything, always taking a scattering of styles and making it work. Sometimes she would wear flowing skirts and scarves with her hair up, then the next day she'd be in jeans and a work shirt or a sun dress and a hat, but she came across as the same person no matter what: serene, impulsive, thoughtful. He could picture the sardonic curve of her mouth, the way she ran a pale hand through her dark hair, and it made him miss her and wish she were home right now to help him pick out just the right stamp to put on the envelope that would carry his story to the editor, to the future, to publication and fame.

He was often tempted to use the standard, plain American flag stamps, certain that most editors would think Okay, this guy's unpretentious, focused on his craft, doesn't go in for a lot of decoration, makes every single word count, businesslike. But then there were others who might think, Who is this one coming from, a John Bircher? Someone who believes showing a glimmer of patriotism on the envelope will sway us in his favor? Then again, other approaches could backfire just as badly. Picasso's

"Guernica" might look fine hanging in a museum, but it was a little callous to paste a miniaturized version on a brown envelope, especially since the stamp bore the legend "USA 32" in one corner. Certain editors would not hesitate to read that the wrong way, to see it as an endorsement on Edwin's part of all kinds of cultural appropriation, although there was also the danger that others would read it as a literal belittlement of a tragedy. A few would be offended by an imagined whiff of political extremism.

If this were a funny story, he might use Felix the Cat or Sally Jesse Raphael, to let the editor know from the moment the mail fell through the slot that here was a writer with a sharp eye for irony. But it wasn't exactly a funny story. It wasn't sad, either. Not a tragedy, but certainly poignant. He settled on a stamp from the American Weeds series: Mexican Primrose. It was in some ways a serious stamp, a vaguely scientific rendering of the flower and its seeds on a plain white background.

He had an equally difficult time deciding how to address the envelope. One school of thought held that it was best to print out a label, creating a tidy, professional appearance. But the publication in question was affiliated with a university, with tweed and elbow patches, loosened ties and sideburns. Sandals. There was the danger that a printed label would trigger the old "here comes another neatly crafted story that takes absolutely no risks" reaction, or the "any story with a printed label is probably sitting on seventy other editors' desks" line of thinking. Normally, Edwin wrote out the addresses by hand, but lately his handwriting had struck him as uneven, almost childish, and he didn't want the editor deciding to go get coffee with the lovely foreign sociology teacher down the hall because the next story in the pile looked like it came from an undergraduate or a diesel mechanic who had taken one creative writing course at the local community college and now fancied himself the next Thomas Wolfe. Once Nia had written out a couple of envelopes for him, not that the stories

had gotten published as a result, but he'd liked her perfectly pro-
portioned G's and softly rounded O's. Her lettering was nothing
fancy, but wonderfully clear and consistent. It was how she was
with him, with everyone. Low-key. She put him at ease. None of
this Hello, how are you today? Not even at the beginning. It was
more like Don't buy that book; it's full of stories about nurses
who poison people and rowboats going over waterfalls. She had
materialized in his favorite bookstore, the only other person in
the aisle, smelling good and looking like a stranger he'd known all
his life. And much later she was that way with his mother at the
restaurant, meaning she made the whole encounter much easier
than Edwin had thought it would be by skipping the formalities,
getting right into questions about Mama's necklace, but no arti-
fice to it, just as she added a little serif to the top of her capital
F not to seem clever but because that was the way she did it. He
wished he could conduct himself as naturally as she did, but he
couldn't, which might have been part of the problem. The best
he could do was try to make it look that way, and with that in
mind Edwin pulled a ruler out of the desk to guide his hand. The
resulting letters were not as effortlessly competent as hers would
have been, but at least the lines in the address didn't slope down
at the ends or vary too much in size.

He banged out the heading of his cover letter in Times
New Roman, which had that stately quality he liked, a sort of ac-
ademic aura, but then it started to look too slick, suggesting that
he was a better word processor than writer. Helvetica, on the
other hand, was overly memo-ish, and the allure of rugged
Courier was too obvious. He wouldn't fall for Geneva, which he'd
once used for an entire story, only to notice as he'd slipped it into
an envelope that Geneva had a sort of young-adult-novel look to
it. Most of the choices were either too cavalier and frank, or too
uptight, snooty. He settled for the time being on Georgia, a larger,
more widely-spaced snooty font, the snootiness tempered by an

open, friendly arrangement. Dear Mr. Peachkin, Edwin typed. Christopher Peachkin. Peachkin. Dear Chris. Christopher. Sir.

It was like the time he and Nia had had a fight about the antiperspirant. It wasn't a fight, he realized. Why think of it that way? She had been getting ready for a quartet rehearsal, standing at the bathroom sink, combing, lotioning, rinsing, deodorizing, putting in her contacts. "Ooh," she'd yelped. "I think I got Smel-Rite in my eye." Edwin sprang into action, moving from the couch to her side in two quick bounds. "Flush with water!" he exclaimed, twisting the faucet handle and cupping his hands. "Come on." He pulled at her arm with one wet hand, trying to get her to bend over the sink.

She yanked her arm away. "It's not that bad," she said, annoyed. "It's just drying up my eye."

"Hm." He peered more closely at her eye. "That would be the alum, I guess. Dries up tears the same way it dries up sweat." Then he went back to his book, and she went to practice. Hours later, they met at the coffeehouse. "How's your eye?" he asked.

"What is it with you and my eye?" she said, with an annoyed laugh. "First you act like it's a medical emergency, then like it's some fascinating laboratory experiment, a human Draize test."

It only got worse. He never knew what to say. Adopt a casual, familiar tone, something like, "Hi, love your magazine, hope you dig the story"? Or more formal: "Enclosed you will find a manuscript entitled 'Drop Kick.' Thank you in advance for your consideration of the enclosed. I have always had the highest regard for your publication." He could picture the editor sitting ramrod straight at his rolltop desk, fountain pen in hand, musty leather-bound tomes lining the shelves above his graying head, a Brandenburg concerto on the Zenith. Or was he checking his teeth in the mirror, gulping the last tablespoon of cold coffee and neatening his ponytail before heading to a class in which he'd take the students out under the big oak and recite e.e. cummings in a nasal voice? If Edwin was careful, he could write the letter innocuously enough that either version of the editor would glean no particular impression from it, leaving the story to get by on its own intrinsic excellence. He typed, "Here is a story called 'Drop Kick.'" See Spot run, he thought. He was much better at speaking to people in person, or so he had thought, but Nia's comments after the serial-killers art opening had made him doubt himself.

It had been her idea to go. She was always cooking up some wacky outing for them, which was one of the things he missed the most. They had gone to the Shrimp and Petroleum Festival in Morgan City one year, and she had asked just about every vendor for shrimp-and-petroleum fettuccine, with the straightest face imaginable. The serial-killers art show was a big deal, featured in the "Hey!" section of the newspaper that morning. "My God," Nia had said after reading about it. "This will generate more than a few letters to the editor. You watch."

He had thought there was a playful shine in her eyes when she said, "Let's go check it out. Tonight, after my church gig." There had been a gleam, no doubt about it.

The gallery was crowded, and Edwin moved with Nia slowly around the perimeter, gawking and chortling right along with everyone else. The art was bad: strange grayish clowns, Christ wearing what appeared to be a crown of beef jerky, and simplistic abstractions resembling drawings from an old geometry textbook. It began to make Edwin a little sick to his stomach, until he had a second plastic glass of champagne. "Can you believe this?" Nia whispered.

"Right," he said, as they approached a man chewing ice. "Wild." The man stood out not only because his face was distorted by crunching, but also because he had his back to the wall. He stood there, whiskey glass in hand, facing not the art but the viewers of the art. "You the artist?" Edwin joked, nodding at the painting by the man's elbow, a pastoral landscape in which the trees and hills looked okay but the red wagon was mangled, made cubist by a lack of skill.

The man snorted. "No, the artist is…."

"No longer with us?" Edwin suggested.

"Right." The man sucked in another cube, rolled his eyes.

That was the kind of spark and connection you couldn't achieve with a letter. How could you ever know whether the addressee grasped what you said, or more crucial, whether they appreciated it? Edwin had thought the ice man had liked his joke, and that Edwin had distinguished himself from the crowd of gawkers as an intelligently cynical critic, but Nia disagreed. She'd been quiet on the way to the car, not responding to his enthusiastic comments about the show. He drove for a few blocks in silence, giving her a chance to speak. At Magazine and Napoleon he murmured, "Thanks, Nia. That was a good idea."

"Ha!" She rolled her window down with angry vigor, then rolled it halfway up. "You got your jollies, didn't you?"

Edwin was amazed. "What? I thought it was, you know, campy."

She turned away from him. "Ugh. Oh, it was sick. It was sick! And on so many levels. It's sick that we live in a society where first of all there are people like that who go around grabbing and killing for years without anyone noticing and who knows how many never get caught and we don't even hear about them, and sick that they even have paintbrushes and easels for them at Angola or wherever they keep them, and even sicker that someone would put together a show of their work like that, and even sicker that people would come to it, and sickest of all that they would just think it was funny." This last phrase was nearly shouted, as the car sat at a stoplight on St. Charles. A heartland tourist standing at the streetcar stop nearby jumped and clutched at his bag, seeming to think her words were directed at him.

Oops, Edwin thought.

"And the one guy that saw through it all, you had to go and insult him," she added.

"Me? Who?"

"The guy with the ice."

"I didn't insult him. I just made a joke."

"Yeah, well, he didn't appreciate it. Didn't you see his face?"

"He was laughing."

"He was glaring!"

Even if Edwin was right and the man was amused, the incident worried him. Why hadn't he noticed Nia's seriousness at the gallery? She had been quiet, but he hadn't detected any angry lowering of the brow or squeezing of his hand. He had misread one, and possibly two people. The experience eroded his confidence a bit, and afterwards he found himself hesitating to pet strange dogs or kid the bank teller about wanting to deposit a million bucks. Maybe for the same reasons, lately he couldn't think of what to say when he called Nia's apartment and she answered, despite the fact that he tried every second or third day. She was always so consistent, lifting the phone with a confident "Hello?" and answering his silence with a contemptuous nasal exhale, then quickly hanging up. She never demanded to know who was there or claimed to know that it was him, never blew a whistle, threatened to call the police, never even banged the phone down. Edwin, on the other hand, had wildly various impulses—to calmly say her name and act as if she'd never thrown a can of Sea Pork tuna at him on their last day together, to narrow his eyes and deliver a curt admonishment, to sob chaotically and hope for tender words—none of which he acted on, sensing that the right choice hadn't occurred to him yet and that all of his impulses were in some way extreme. Externally, at least, his calls were just as consistent as her responses: absolute silence. He was careful not to breathe, to have no appliances running in the background. How do I end this? he wondered now. He considered punctuating it with something splashy and incoherent, urbane, to make himself seem so completely self-possessed and certain of victory that there would be no hesitation. Or cryptic and casual, a vague hieroglyphic to suggest his mind was much more occupied with writing stories than with cover-letter politics. Should he use the same signature he scratched onto the bottoms of checks, or a specially reserved monogram? He knew it made no difference, but felt that it did. Acceptance or rejection couldn't possibly ride on the way he signed his name. Although who would have ever thought that the way he rode an old Honda scooter would have anything to do with Nia's leaving him?

She claimed it was because she was tired of taking the bus to rehearsals and reluctant to inconvenience him by getting rides, but later he wondered if it was because she knew she would be moving out before long and would need her own transportation. In any case, one Sunday morning she scanned the "Two-Wheeled Motorized Conveyances" section of the classified ads, made a few calls, and announced that a man named Les was bringing his old Honda scooter over for her to test drive in twenty minutes. She invited Edwin to sit out on the front stoop to wait for Les, and even suggested they bring glasses of iced tea, her good mood giving Edwin hope that the feeling he'd had lately of mutually suppressed bile was bogus.

Les came cruising up on the tomato-red scooter, helmet tipped back, one hand loose on the throttle, the other putting a cigarette to his mouth. "All right," he said happily, dismounting and stomping on the butt in one smooth motion. "I'm Les. This is the scooter. You must be Nia."

"And he's Edwin," Nia said.

Les took off the helmet and gave her a rundown of the simple machine's features: hand brake, foot brake, shifter, throttle, headlight. "Try it," he suggested to Nia.

"You first, Edwin," Nia said. "I haven't ridden one of these in years."

Edwin shrugged and swung his leg over the seat. He gingerly toed the scooter into gear and buzzed slowly down the drive, then halfheartedly drove down the block and back. "Yeah," he said to Nia when he had returned. "It works."

Nia was smirking, trying not to laugh. "I'm sorry," she murmured, ignoring Les's demonstration of proper choke operation. "You were sitting up so straight, like this." She stuck her butt out and held her arms out straight, pursing her lips comically.

Edwin just nodded, but inside he felt his heart stoning over. He knew that in such a situation some people would exact revenge immediately, would make a joke about the way she asked two or three times where the brake was and acted surprised when the twisting of the throttle produced an anemic revving. He wasn't the type to take an eye for an eye, a posture-lampoon for a posture-lampoon, despite the way she hunched forward nervously on the bike, knees and elbows thrown out. Somewhere in some celestial ledger he no doubt earned a few points for showing such restraint.

She bought the scooter for four hundred dollars, and Les threw in the bright blue helmet for free. The roof didn't fall in until later. All day she spoke happily about the scooter, romanticizing its utility, loyalty, efficiency, and more than once she went out to look at it, mentioning taking it for a spin without doing so. Edwin just played along and tried to get through the book he was reading. Finally she appeared in the living room with the helmet under her arm, said she was just going to try it out for a few minutes, get some practice. He encouraged her to be careful.

Five minutes later she was back. She walked in with a red face, helmet still strapped on, holding her left wrist gingerly.

"What happened?" he asked, alarmed at the quiver in her lip.

"I was trying to turn the corner and I got those things mixed up and it wouldn't stop," she told him, her voice reedy with ill-suppressed anguish. "I ran into a 'Slow Children' sign. The people sitting on the porch saw the whole thing. I think I broke my arm."

"Where's the bike?" Edwin asked. Later he would realize that her sudden look of composure came from anger, and that she showed some restraint of her own in giving a straight answer.

"It's still there."

"Let me look at your arm," Edwin said gently, but much too late. He thought her arm looked okay, and offered to get her an ice pack; she insisted that it hurt and that she needed to go to the emergency room. He explained that broken bones caused immediate and acute swelling; she reiterated. After cajoling her into at least trying the ice and extracting a grudging admission that it felt better, he retrieved the scooter from up the street, noting the new kink in its handlebars. A few minutes later he told her he had to go to work, and she replied with a brusque "Fine."

Hours later, Edwin came home to find Nia sitting on the couch with a plaster cast from thumb to elbow, and that was pretty much it, except for a little tearful shouting and throwing of tuna. What he remembered most clearly, though, was that image of her test driving the scooter, arms and legs awkwardly akimbo. That was her signature, her final flourish, and he knew his ramrod-straight posture on the Honda was at the bottom of the page on which she had written her memories of their life together.